St. Mark's Ave.: Life in Old Brooklyn

Jos. C. Donato

Ekstasis Multimedia
Blairstown, New Jersey

Ekstasis Multimedia: www.booksandbrush.net

St. Mark's Ave.: Life in Old Brooklyn/Jos. C. Donato
Blairstown, New Jersey: Ekstasis Multimedia, LLC, 2014
ISBN-13: 978-0615917146
ISBN-10: 0615917143

Book design: Marlaina Donato
Author photo: Marlaina Donato

For my Dad, for his captivating descriptions of people and places that recalled his boyhood adventures in a bygone era.

Author's Note

It was the era following the First World War in the Park Slope section of Brooklyn, New York, a time when some streets were still lit with gas lamps and paved with cobblestone. In this part of the city, thousands of recently-arrived immigrants from Italy had settled. This wave of immigration had begun in the 1880s and continued into the 1920s. The influx of newcomers was somehow absorbed as the Irish and Germans before them. In particular, the Italian and Jewish arrivals made their homes in adjoining sections of Brooklyn and drifted into pockets primarily occupied by people of similar culture. The resulting increase in neighborhoods added to the ever-expanding new borough. My father Dominick, his parents, and siblings settled in one of these areas. His father, Giuseppe—an eighteen-year-old shoemaker—had arrived in America in 1887 seeking a better life. He returned to Italy years later and married Carolina, his boyhood sweetheart, and brought her to New York at the turn of the century with their firstborn son. My father was the fourth eldest of the boys and third son to be born in Brooklyn. This story is based on his life and experiences during a more innocent time in American history.

A Summer Day Long Ago

The distinct rhythm of the milk wagon broke the early silence of the sleepy neighborhood. The sun had just risen on that warm July morning in 1918 as eight-year-old Dominick was pleasantly awakened by familiar sounds of the street coming through his bedroom window. *Clack, clack, clack*, the iron-shod hooves of a slow-moving horse struck the hard cobblestone. Though it disturbed the serenity of the morning, the sound was comforting. The wagon stopped at intervals as it made its way along St. Mark's Ave.

The boy lay back with his hands clasped behind his head and paused to savor the moment. A smile flickered across his round face when he heard low voices in the kitchen.

Carolina, his energetic mother, was preparing breakfast for her reluctant, slowly-emerging children. The aromas of freshly baked rolls and coffee drifted into his bedroom that he shared with his younger brother Carly. Tempted enough, Dominick gave in and dressed quickly.

He entered the dim kitchen where his parents and much older brother Jimmy were just finishing their breakfast. They all turned and smiled as Jimmy greeted Dominick, "Say, Dom, why are you getting up so early? It's summer and there's no school. Oh, I know! You don't want to miss anything, eh?" He tousled his hair.

"Nope, I just have a lot of things to do today."

"So, you have a heavy schedule?" chided Jimmy with a wink, his green eyes warm with affection.

"Don't tease him. Maybe he does have some things to take care of," their father Giuseppe said. Dominick brushed off his brother's teasing and dug into the buttered rolls. Just then a few high-pitched voices sounded from beneath the kitchen window. They turned out to be a few neighborhood boys calling on Dominick.

"Hey, Dom! You gonna sleep all day? Come on, already!" his young friend Danny yelled.

"Yeah, come on, we ain't got all day!" added Joey.

Dominick, a little annoyed, got up and went to the window. "Hold on to your shirts! I'll be out as soon as I can."

"Dominick, why do you hang around with those ruffians?" his father interjected, "they're always up to no good."

"Oh, Pop, these guys are alright. They're my friends," he

said in defense. In a few minutes, Dominick joined his two friends and they all walked toward the corner to meet up with the other boys. It was a meeting place for all the kids in the neighborhood where they conjured up activities for the day, both good and not so good. "Hey, you guys, whatja wanna do? Got any ideas?" asked Bach, as he scuffed the ground with his shoe and his dark brown hair fell into his even darker eyes.

"Let's go to Prospect Park. It's a nice day, and we could go around the lake," suggested Henry, straightening his corduroy cap.

"Eh, we did that last week. Let's do something else," Red said. "All right, I got a good idea. Today is Tuesday, right? That means Rocco the vegetable guy will be coming soon. Let's have some fun." His blue eyes lit up with devilish enthusiasm.

"Good idea," Dominick agreed, "Let's get ready for him."

The plotting youths walked to the middle of the block and then split up. Half went to one side of the street while the others went to the opposite side. They took a seat on the front steps of the houses that lined the street and waited for the unsuspecting peddler. To pass the time, Red took out a deck of cards, and soon they were all engrossed in the game. As the good-natured peddler turned his wagon onto St. Mark's Ave. he began his rhythmic sales pitch and sang about his wares. Luckily, the Neapolitan possessed a strong, pleasant voice. The fresh fruits and vegetables had been purchased earlier that morning at the large produce market in lower Manhattan, and the variety was impressive.

Instantly, the women of the neighborhood appeared at their windows and doorways. Some shouted down to inquire about the ripeness of the tomatoes and eggplants. The stocky, mustached Rocco halted his wagon close to the curb and in no time was surrounded by would-be customers. The women pushed their way to the sides of the wagon to haggle prices. Then of course, the proverbial questions, "Are they fresh and how much a pound?" These old-world women tried to pick the choicest of the produce. One or two would go so far as to sample a peach or a large bunch of plump grapes after which it was not uncommon for them to criticize, "Too sour!" yet continue to eat whatever was left in their hands. At that point, Rocco would throw his arms up and shoo them away.

"No toucha! I'll tell you if they are sweeta. Please, no toucha!"

"Rocco, will you please put these potatoes in the bag. I can't wait here all day," Dominick's mother interrupted, tired of waiting for the potatoes to be put on the scale. "I have clothes to wash and a house to clean."

"Si si, Signora, right away. But I have to watch those two over there because they will steal the eyes right outta my head!"

Meanwhile, across the street, Dominick's buddies Joey and Henry eyed the back-end of the wagon. They planned their means of escape with a nice ripe cantaloupe. "I took them the last time, Joey. Now it's your turn," Henry challenged him.

"Look, I'd rather chance it when he pulls away from the curb," Joey decided. Henry thought for a while and then agreed.

"There he goes. Now's your chance," Henry whispered after a few moments passed. Joey hesitated for a second then dashed toward the moving wagon. He ran, grabbed the side, and swung himself up but jumped down again just as quickly. "What happened?" Henry asked, looking disappointed. Joey walked toward Henry a little annoyed with himself.

"Darn, the crate was nailed closed. I couldn't grab anything." Discouraged, they shuffled over to a nearby stoop and sat down. Chappie, a stray dog the neighborhood kids had adopted, came over and greeted them.

"Aw, gee, nothin' to do again. I wish we were rich. We could go to the country for the whole summer," complained Henry.

"Whatja kickin' about? You have a lot more than poor little Chappie. You have a mother and a father and sisters who care about you. Poor Chappie doesn't have anyone in particular to look after him," Joey said, as he put an arm around the short-haired, affectionate dog.

"Well at least," Henry added, "when Chappie does something wrong, he don't get punished like we do."

"I would still radda have my mother and father than be Chappie," Joey reasoned.

"I guess yer right," Henry conceded.

Suddenly, they heard some sort of commotion from the end of the street, and the boys hastily made their way toward the disturbance. Nudging their way through the small crowd, Dominick and Red got there first to see who was involved in the altercation. To Dominick's surprise, his younger brother Carly was squaring off with a much larger youth named Tommy.

It had apparently all stemmed from a game of Ringolevio, one of the many popular games played in the city neighborhoods. Carly grabbed Tommy by the shirt in attempt to catch him, and when Tommy pulled away, the shirt ripped from the neck to the waist and hung down to the back of his knees. Carly, who was mild-mannered and younger, apologized. "Gee, Tommy, I didn't mean to do that."

"I ought to bust you in the mouth," Tommy decided. He had a reputation for being a bully and scaring his opponents. The crowd didn't help matters and were goading Tommy into a fight. "You didn't mean it? You trying to kid me? You did that on poypus. Put up your hands!"

Some of the older boys were eager to see a brawl and hoped Tommy would get his lumps. They started to prod Carly to fight back. "Go ahead, Carly, take him on! He's only a big bag of wind," one of the boys egged him on.

One of the bystanders quickly became a self-appointed referee as the boys began to square off. Tommy threw a fast punch at Carly who tried to duck, but the blow caught him on top of the head. "Now cut it out, Tommy," Carly said, "I don't want to fight you."

"Oh, you don't do ya? Well, here's another!" Tommy swung again, and this time Carly was able to avoid the punch. Carly swung when Tommy moved past him and caught him with a hard right on the chin. The surprised bully immediately went down with a befuddled expression on his face. He got up from the ground and went after Carly who was dancing around waiting for him. Tommy lunged at him, this time Carly sidestepping and hitting him flush in the nose. Blood poured profusely down his face and onto the front of his shirt, but he kept on sparring.

"Cheese it, the cops!" someone yelled, and the crowd dispersed in haste. The brawling boys were quickly ushered into a nearby tenement hallway where they waited until the police left. Tommy and Carly then returned to the street and promptly resumed where they had left off. Once again, Tommy was able to throw the first punch, a short jab that got Carly in the nose. Carly soon realized that he was bleeding, too.

"Carly, here comes your mother!" somebody shouted. Carolina, a formidable woman, pushed her way through the small mob and grabbed her son by the arm and forcibly escorted him toward home.

"Atta boy, Carly! Good fight! You showed him!" came another voice from the crowd of bystanders. Carly felt like a hero because he had stood up to a bully and given more than he had received. Dominick and his friends were all keyed up as they walked toward the corner talking about the fight. "There was sure a lot of blood," Henry commented. "Hey, look...there's the rest of the gang!" He pointed toward the corner. "The last one to get down to the corner's a bum!" With that, Dominick darted off with the others close at his heels.

"Ah, you got a head start, you fink!" Joey said, running faster to keep up. The boys sprinted past three women in deep conversation near the neighborhood stables. Suddenly, Henry, who was running as fast as he could to catch up, slipped on a stone and careened uncontrollably toward the women. They fortunately caught a glimpse of the falling youth and were able to avoid a collision. Henry, though, was not as lucky and sprawled into the gutter. Adding insult to injury, the three women used adjectives that did not compliment his heritage. Poor Henry's timing couldn't have been worse, for minutes before, a number of horses had just paused before entering the stable and relieved themselves at the same exact spot. Needless to say, when he realized what he had fallen into, he was quite agitated with himself. He tried to brush himself off and continued to hear remarks from the irritated women whom he had almost taken down with him. Not knowing anything better to say, Henry looked at them and remarked, "Aw, why don't ya go fly a kite? Wadda ya want, blood?"

Looking quite disheveled, he limped toward the corner where all of his friends had gathered to laugh at his latest bad luck. As he approached them, he heard Dominick say, "Hey, Henry, what a dive. A perfect half gainer." They all kept laughing and rehashing Henry's zany mishaps. It finally came to an end when each boy retreated home to dinner with hopes of being able to meet up once again on the corner.

Duke and Prince

Along with Dominick's family of four brothers and a sister, there were also two more integral personalities. A furry white Spitz named Duke and a mutt named Prince. The older Duke was a constant companion to Carolina, shadowing her every movement and making his residence not far from the coal stove in the busy kitchen. Due to his close proximity and gentleness to the family, Duke was pampered and spoiled. He was always there when everyone woke up in the morning and retired for the night, and only ventured outside when necessary.

Prince, on the other hand, was smaller, dark-haired, and short-tempered. He would ask to go out early in the morning and only return for supper in the evening. The neighborhood and beyond was his domain. He was a rough and tumble dog with little fear. To the astonishment of the rest of the family, this independent creature favored only Dominick who had a way with him.

One day Dominick and his friends were engaged in a game of cards with boys from another neighborhood. Things were going well until one of them became irritated when he kept losing. He promptly broke up the game and falsely accused Dominick and his pals of cheating. The other boys left angrily and didn't look back. Dominick and his friends continued to play cards. Within a half hour, the boy who thought he had been cheated came back with a few cohorts accompanied by a large Italian Mastiff on a leash. The dog boldly pranced toward them as Dominick—anticipating a confrontation—looked knowingly at his friends. Bach stood up and questioned, "You're back? Wadda ya want?"

"We're back to even up," the so-called wronged boy remarked.

"We told you, nobody cheated. You lost fair and square. Whadda ya want, our blood?" Danny rebuked.

"You know, that's a good idea," the boy with the dog said, as he dropped the leash and ordered, "Sic 'em, Brutus!" Without hesitation, the dog bounded and grabbed Red's arm and brought the boy to the ground. Dominick and the others started kicking the vicious dog from behind. Brutus released Red instantly, went after Bach, and bit him in the leg. His pants ripped and exposed his bleeding flesh. Horrified, Dominick managed to clutch a discarded broom and swung at the ravaging animal. The blow hit the dog's back. The surprised Mastiff yelped and let go of Bach's leg. The dog then swung around, snarled and jumped onto Dominick who collapsed under the dog's heavy weight. Instinctively, Brutus went for Dominick's throat, but the boy managed to have the presence of mind to raise his right arm to block the attack. The mad dog grabbed Dominick's arm and pulled him further into the street. His helpless friends and passersby screamed at the determined beast. The loud yells for help got the attention of Dominick's dog, Prince, who was at the other end of the block. He heard the boy's cries of distress, and with ears standing straight up, cocked his head and instantly launched into a full run straight down the middle of the street. Oblivious to everything and everyone, the dog dashed toward the scene.

The attacking Mastiff was still on top of Dominick when Prince lunged at the larger dog's hind leg. Caught off guard, Brutus quickly let go of Dominick and pivoted around. Prince crouched down as Brutus, twice his size, charged toward his challenging intruder intending to pounce. Prince remained crouched as Brutus charged forward. Just as the Mastiff was about to spring on top of him, Prince sprung upward and gripped Brutus by the throat. The stunned animal tried to shake loose from Prince's hold and couldn't, but Prince was not going to back down and let go. Again, Brutus tried to swing himself free, but the attempt was futile. The big dog became desperate and realized that he was in a death grip. After minutes of struggling, the Mastiff finally whimpered and slumped to the ground on his side in total submission.

Dominick and a number of men were able to coax Prince to release his hold, which he did with great reluctance. At the same time, the boy who had started the altercation hustled his dog away from the scene with humiliation.

Had it not been for his brave, small dog, Dominick and his friends would have been severely mauled. As it was, they had suffered wounds from the attack, but fortunately, within the week, all recovered enough to resume their rambunctious lives.

From that time, Prince was lauded as a hero—the David who had defeated Goliath. With gratitude, families in the neighborhood brought Prince special treats for days, which he happily devoured.

Briganti's

At one of the four corners stood a popular gathering place called Briganti's, a saloon named after the owner. Typical of others of its kind in the early 20th century, the bar had swinging doors and sawdust floors. A number of brass spittoons were strategically located at the base of a long bar which was always crowded with customers. Briganti was a burley, fair-minded, and no-nonsense individual. He was assisted by a much younger man who helped tend bar. An integral part of the atmosphere was Bull, an Italian mastiff that slept with one eye open to watch the goings-on. His intimidating presence was unavoidable and was an untested guardian of his realm. Dominick, Red, and the other boys could not help themselves from frequenting the stone steps outside the saloon doors. There they were allowed to sit and play cards as long as they did not interfere with the comings and goings of customers; another condition was to never enter the establishment under any circumstance. The boys readily complied, for they liked playing on the wide, flat steps. An advantage to occupying the steps into the evening was having sufficient light coming from under the swinging doors which enabled them to continue playing cards. Another added attraction was the boisterous chatter of customers having a good time. There were times when situations became heated and were fanned by the consumption of spirits. Fights were not uncommon but soon quelled by Briganti and his Mastiff companion, Bull. If the atmosphere turned hostile, Bull's ears would instinctively point forward toward the commotion. Bull would slowly raise himself from his proverbial position at the end of the bar and zero in on the direction of the disturbance. The majority of incidents required only one look and one low growl to stop an altercation before it had a chance to escalate. If this was not enough, a nod from Briganti would signal Bull to go after the rowdy perpetrators. After such an incident and all returned to normal, Bull would resume his restful position at the foot of the bar. Despite his appearance and watchful nature, he was a gentle animal and during slow times in the tavern, would walk under the swinging doors and join the boys playing cards on the steps. The imposing dog sitting alongside the young men was a sight to see. He was a different dog with them, and Dominick and his buddies could not help but love the gentle beast. Many a time a customer entering the bar would take a bewildered glance at the massive dog sitting with the kids and shake his head.

Briganti's was a bone of contention with Giuseppe; he did not like his son choosing such a hang-out and worried about Dominick's welfare and the bad example of the type of men who frequented the establishment. Because of this, one of the boys would alert Dominick to hide when they saw his father approaching until Giuseppe was out of sight.

The bar attracted a myriad of personalities, including men of substantial position who would meet there to close deals. Others were tradesmen who congregated in the hopes of offering their services for sales or for barter. At the lower end were day laborers who looked for work with construction contractors and builders. The saddest of the lot were those who could not work because of age and those without hope who wandered into unfortunate, derelict behavior.

There seemed to always be something interesting going on at Briganti's, for example, the common sight of the weekly beer delivery. The boys considered themselves fortunate if they were there when the long flatbed arrived. The heavy chain-driven vehicle would occupy a good portion of the street, and two strapping men donned in leather aprons and heavy gloves would exit the front cab. They would then pull themselves up onto the flatbed and begin to maneuver the lashed wooden barrels of beer. The onlookers would be impressed by the strong men jostling and flipping the casks onto their sides with ease before rolling them down on two thick planks to the street. They would then tip them up onto a handcart and roll them to the front steps where they lifted them into the saloon. The men repeated this process three or four times while the neighborhood boys stood close by. They were amazed by their brute strength and the way they made it look effortless.

One Friday night after a busy evening, three strangers entered the bar just before midnight after the crowd had already dwindled. A few regulars looked up at them but then returned to their conversations. One of the strangers sat down at a table near the front door, and the other two approached the bar at opposite sides. Briganti had his back to them as he cleaned glasses. He felt something wasn't right when he turned and faced one of the men. He then noticed the other stranger at the other end of the bar. "What can I get you to drink?" he asked him.

"I'll have a beer," he responded. Briganti reached down under the bar and pretended to get a glass, but instead grabbed a shot gun and pointed it at the stranger in front of him who had already drawn a pistol.

"You'd better get out while you can still walk," Briganti warned.

"I will, as soon as you empty the money out of the register," the man demanded. At the opposite end of the bar, the other man also brandished a gun as back-up.

"Bull!" Briganti yelled out, "Go get 'em!" In a split second, the dog that had been lying only a few feet from one of the intruders pounced on the unsuspecting man without warning. He sunk his teeth into his arm, and the surprised man dropped the gun. The other man confronting Briganti turned to look at his cohort being mauled. Briganti took advantage of his distraction. He reached across the bar and hit the would-be thief across the face with the shotgun barrel, and the man tumbled unconscious to the floor. At that point, the third cohort seated by the front door bolted out of the tavern. Briganti then ordered Bull to release the man. The dog heeded his command and let go. "Bull, go get him!" Briganti added, pointing to the door. Obedient Bull darted out and chased after the thief. The robber sprinted, but he was no match for the dog, who within seconds leapt onto his back. The desperate man sprawled onto the street as his gun flew out of his grasp. Bull ferociously latched onto his leg and wouldn't let go. Back at the saloon, a couple of customers apprehended the would-be robber who Bull had released, and Briganti ran out to catch up with Bull. Fortunately for the thief, Briganti ordered Bull to stop.

News traveled fast, and police arrived to round up the wounded thieves and escort them away. When Briganti and his dog returned to the bar the remaining customers and friends happily gathered around them. They all knew that if not for Bull, the outcome would have been far different, and the amount of personal injury and financial damage would have been significant.

The following day everyone had heard of the news of how Bull demonstrated such protectiveness and loyalty, and for a while, he was the hero of the neighborhood.

Extraordinary Luck

When Dominick came into the world, he was born with the embryonic veil intact. According to cultural superstition, it was considered an auspicious and rare event. The midwife in attendance insisted that his parents keep it for good fortune. The membrane was kept to dry out and turn to dust then placed in a small leather pouch so it could be worn around the neck for luck. Carolina told Dominick to never lose it or sell it to anyone, especially seamen who were particularly interested in possessing its powers. On more than one occasion, men sought to buy the rarity when Dominick was seen sporting it around his neck. Once, he was offered as much as five hundred dollars but refused to part with it.

Young Dominick *did* have phenomenal, unexplainable

good fortune, including the time his dog Prince appeared out of nowhere and saved him and his friends from being mauled. Another incident occurred when Dominick borrowed his friend Frankie's brand new bike. Frankie pleaded with him to be very careful with it, for his father would be very angry with him if anything should happen.

Shrugging off his friend's advice, Dominick hopped on the new bike and took off. Frankie became quite upset and suspected something had gone wrong when Dominick did not return within a reasonable time. By chance, Frankie's father happened to walk by and saw that his son was upset and without his bike. He asked Frankie what had happened, and the boy told him he had loaned it to one of his friends. Just then, Dominick appeared half a block away and motioned to Frankie and his father to come toward him. They approached Dominick and saw that he was blocking their view from something behind him. He finally stepped aside, and they were shocked to see the twisted mass of metal which used to be Frankie's new bike. Dominick apologized and told them that a speeding Model T hit him broadside and never stopped. He had been catapulted from the bike and made a soft landing in a row of nearby hedges. Miraculously, he had survived without a scratch. Frankie's father tenderly put his arm on Dominick's shoulder. Somewhat relieved, the man was more concerned about Dominick's wellbeing than the fate of the bike. Judging from the destruction of the bike, it was obvious he could have been hurt severely, or worse.

Dominick was not reprimanded, and Frankie did not

suffer from any repercussions. Dominick's luck was once again evident.

Many of the neighborhood boys were very industrious and would run errands for the local people. Some delivered groceries for those who were not able to get to stores. Others would sweep sidewalks for business owners and help deliver ice to second and third floor tenements. Their efforts were usually rewarded with a nickel or a dime, and some instances, a whole quarter. Therefore, they always had small change in their pockets which they would spend on ice cream, penny candies, and going to the movies once a week.

One Saturday Dominick, Joey, Bach, and Red went to the movie theater in downtown Brooklyn. They went to see a double feature with Western star Tom Mix. There was an intermission after the first movie and hundreds of excited, screaming kids had finally settled down. At that time, the theater's manager took the stage to pick a winner, lottery-style for a prize. Their ticket stubs had been ripped in half—one part kept by the theater and the other by the customer. Alongside the manager was a large drum filled with ticket stubs. The prize to be given away that Saturday was a boy's size Buffalo Bill-style leather fringe jacket. Hordes of kids were ecstatic about the possibility of winning such a prize. The manager raised his arms in an attempt to quiet the rambunctious audience. He proceeded to turn the handle of the drum for a good mix. After a few rotations, he reached in to pull the winning ticket. In anticipation of winning, the crowd of youths became quiet. The manager smiled and slowly announced the numbers of the winning ticket. There was a hush over the crowd as everyone checked their stubs. Joey was the first to realize he hadn't won and shook his head. Bach and Red quickly followed suit. They looked around the audience for the lucky stiff who had the winning ticket. Meanwhile, Dominick also shook his head, but in disbelief. He stood up with the winning number and raced to the stage to collect his prize. He was obviously the envy of all the kids in the theater.

Later, when he returned to the neighborhood, his friends swarmed around him with admiration. After Saturday's happy commotion wore off, Dominick and the others resumed their routine.

The following week was brutally hot, and the city sent workers into the surrounding neighborhoods to turn on the hire hydrants. Sprays were attached that offered a larger area to be doused with a fine shower. This was brief and welcome relief for the children of the borough and would be a weekly event through August. Happy kids and their dogs relished in the delightful treat.

The sweltering weather took its toll on the residents of the uninsulated, pre-Civil War tenements. After three or four hours, to the dismay of all the kids, workers were ordered to turn the hydrants off.

The remainder of the week passed without much excitement. When Friday rolled around, the boys discussed going to the movies again. Tarzan of the Apes and the Adventures of Zorro were playing the next day at the same theater they had gone to the week before.

On Saturday, Dominick and his friends were joined by Goose and Danny, two others from the neighborhood. Goose, nicknamed for his exceptionally long neck, ran to the trolley first, and to the dismay of the motorman, the boys all skipped a ride. Once at the theater, they purchased tickets and somehow managed to sit in the same seats they had occupied the week before.

At the conclusion of the Tarzan movie, once again during intermission, the manager of the theater prepared to give away another prize—a leather-bound, eight-volume set of American history. As always, he rotated the drum, reached in, and withdrew the winning number. Dominick and the other boys from St. Mark's Ave. all glanced at their stubs with high hopes. One by one, they shook their heads. Again, the only boy not shaking his head was Dominick. He looked at his pals and said, "You're not going to believe this, but I just won again!"

"You gotta be kiddin'! Not again!" Red wailed. Dominick jumped out of his seat and ran down the aisle toward the stage. The manager's face dropped when he saw Dominick making his way up the steps. He quickly went to the side of the bewildered man.

"Is this a joke?" the manager asked in disbelief. Dominick showed him the ticket.

"I've won it fair and square." The flustered man had no choice but to reluctantly hand over the prize. Dominick grabbed the heavy strapped books, one stack in each hand, and barely managed to walk back to his green-eyed friends. They still couldn't believe what they had witnessed and called him Houdini.

When the boys returned to the neighborhood, news of Dominick's good fortune spread like wildfire. For days they called him Mr. Lucky, and it was well-deserved.

Mischief at the Feast

There was an air of happy anticipation among everyone in the neighborhood; that week the Feast of Our Lady of Mt. Carmel was to be celebrated. Dominick and his friends worked especially hard at odd jobs to save enough money to splurge at the festive event.

The local business owners were especially joyful, for it brought many other people from other sections of Brooklyn to enjoy the festivities. Colored lights were strung from poles, and large canvas tents were erected to accommodate the crowds. Vendors of all kinds added to the atmosphere. They sold a variety of items, from religious articles to an array of foodstuffs. Italian sandwiches made of sausage, sweet fried peppers and eggplant, and spicy meatballs were quite popular, and for those with a sweet tooth- cannoli, zapola, colorful Italian cookies, spumoni, and tangy lemon ice were available.

This gala event was held on a Saturday evening and all through Sunday up until midnight. Early in the morning on the first day, the vendors chose their places to set up their booths, and St. Mark's Ave. was blocked to traffic between Troy and Schenectady.

All the boys and girls were intrigued to see the way the vendors methodically set up the displays of their wares. Dominick and Red were particularly interested in a short, mustached Neapolitan named Angelo. They remembered him from the years before and found him very comical as he inflated his colorful balloons. Both boys conjured up a mischievous plot. Red's older brother owned a B.B gun and Red knew where he kept it. He and Dominick noticed that Angelo and his balloons were set up curbside very close to a billboard that stood ten feet above the sidewalk. They also observed that the festival lights were strung a few feet below the top of it, therefore, when the lights were on, Angelo could not see beyond them. Dominick and Red walked behind and tried to figure out how to stand on the wooden two by four frame and discovered it could easily be done. Best of all, they would not be seen after dark.

Before the festival officially began, both boys went home to eat supper and promised to not stay out too late. Once Dominick returned to the celebration, he made his way behind the billboard and waited for his friend as the lights were switched on. Red soon arrived with the B.B. gun, and the two little pranksters climbed up the back of the billboard. They positioned themselves and waited until it was darker. From their undetectable perch, they watched Angelo's unintentional comical mannerisms with amusement as he sold balloons. His overly-sweet politeness and broken English was a hilarious skit right out of Vaudeville. The boys did all they could to contain their laughter without revealing their position.

At last, it was dark enough to carry out their mischievous prank. Within a few minutes, a husband and wife walked up to Angelo to purchase a balloon for their young son. "Gooda evening. It's a wondaful nighta! You wanna balloon, you nisa boy?" The couple nodded, and with that, Angelo reached over to the bunch of balloons tied to his pushcart and chose a red one. He was in process of handing it to the boy when it suddenly popped. Anxious to please, Angelo said, "Somatimes you get a badda one, but that's okay." As he reached for another balloon, the two snickering culprits readied themselves for another shot. The background of music from the street musicians was enough to drown out the muffled sound of the B.B. gun when the balloon was hit. The stunned Angelo remained standing with the limp string in his hand and stared in disbelief. He somehow was able to maintain some kind of composure. "Coulda be, itsa the birds," the vendor reasoned, "but no, itsa nighttime. Son uvva gunna, itsa still okay. I give you anotha." He untied the third balloon but before handing it over to the befuddled little boy, he looked left and right in anticipation of something happening. He paused a few seconds and when nothing occurred, shrugged his shoulders and said, "Well, I guessa there are no more birdsa around." Just as he was cautiously handing the balloon to the pouting boy, it popped. This time Angelo could not hold back his

31

frustration. "Sonna ma bitcha, if I ever get my handsa around you necka, I'lla kill you!" Meanwhile, the couple and their son quickly left the irate vendor, turning to look at Angelo going berserk. He took the remainder of the balloons and destroyed all of them, shouting, "Nowa you bastids, you have no mora balloonsa to break. Howda you lika dat?" Dominick and Red laughed uncontrollably and were barely able to climb down the back of the billboard. They found a place to hide the B.B. gun and waited a while until the coast was clear. When it was safe, they returned to the street and blended into the crowd. After walking to the middle of the block, the boys passed Angelo who was still flaying his arms and telling another vendor about his unusual bad luck.

People had paid two dollars to sit on the grand stands and listen to Italian musical favorites and partake from an assortment of cold cut sandwiches which were placed on trays between the bleachers. Dominick suggested they go over to listen to the band and Red agreed halfheartedly. The always-hungry boys devised a way of sneaking a sandwich or two. The grand stands were crowded with adults enjoying the music, but Dominick and Red figured out a way to climb beneath the seats. There, while balancing themselves on the framework, they reached between the spectators. Dominick was the first to successfully snatch a sandwich between the people's legs. Red's attempt to do the same was also fruitful, but he decided to go for another. His hand went into the tray and managed to grab the additional sandwich, but as he withdrew, a larger hand grasped his. Red immediately screamed as he was pulled through the spacing beneath the seats. The strong man threatened to bring the boy down to the local police precinct.

Unnoticed, Dominick climbed down and raced toward home when he heard his friend yelling. When he reached his house he told his father what had happened and asked for his help. Giuseppe was well respected in the neighborhood, so without delay, he headed toward the festival with Dominick in tow.

Upon arrival, Red was still in the grip of the offended man who was adamant about having the boy arrested. Giuseppe approached them and pled a good case for Red to not be brought in, emphasizing that it would be a sin to have a young man begin life with a record. Fortunately, he struck a chord with the man who also had children of his own. Things calmed down, and it was agreed that it would not go any further, thanks to Giuseppe's passionate plea. Red was forever grateful.

Harvest Days Upstate

News circulated in the neighborhood that farmers upstate were seeking families who would pick crops for free room and board during a three-week period in August. Carolina was very much in favor for such a venture, as it was an opportunity to get the family away from the sweltering city heat. Other families they knew had already accepted and signed up for the commitment.

Carolina, her boys, and her daughter Rose were all excited about the trip. The only obstacle would be to convince Giuseppe to go along with it.

One night after supper, the entire family gathered around the table to discuss the opportunity's merits. It was a requirement that everyone over the age of twelve would work in the fields, and Giuseppe had reservations about this. Due to his work, he would not be going and would only be able to join them on weekends. Most of the fathers of the other families were to do likewise. However, after much pressure from the children, Giuseppe finally consented.

Before they were to leave for the farm, the Donatos began to gather clothes, canned goods, dried beans and rice, and a few favored cast iron skillets. A few days before the trip, the entire neighborhood was in happy anticipation of their new undertaking. Since most of the families were also going, it was a happy, party-like atmosphere.

Finally, Monday morning arrived, and all six participating families assembled at the corner of St. Mark's and Troy. To the onlooker, it must have been an odd exodus of women and children armed with a variety of suitcases and burlap sacks.

They began their trek through the humid city streets to the subway. Curious stares were cast in their direction. Oblivious to what others might have been thinking, the jovial, easy-going bunch continued on their journey. They arrived at Grand Central Station terminal and were directed to the train that was to take them to their rural destination. For most of the migrating families, it was the first time they had ridden on a train other than the subway. It was a pleasant novelty as all vied to get a window seat.

Soon the northbound train left the bustling city. The scenery changed quickly, from concrete to greener open spaces. Houses became fewer, and streets gave way to breezy fields and meadows. It was all to the delight of the children who had never been further than the city limits. Most of them had their small noses pressed against the windows to not miss anything. A new pastoral scene emerged with every mile traveled. The winding train track crossed over fast-moving rivers and rugged ravines, through seemingly endless, dense woods. Lush pastures dotted with grazing cows, sheep, and horses captivated the young travelers.

Time passed unnoticed as most of the adults dozed off to the train's calming rhythm. Their slumber was broken by the conductor moving through the cars and informing the passengers of the next stop which was the town where the families would get off. The heavy steam engine slowed down as it approached the rural station. Everyone scrambled and gathered their belongings as they prepared to exit.

Once the train came to a halt, the anxious passengers swiftly scampered down the steps to the station platform. The sight of the somewhat disheveled group resembled a bunch of refugees from a destitute land. It was of no matter, for their spirits were of hope and jubilant determination. The undeniably sweet smell of newly-mown grass was a welcome change from the dense air of the city.

Dominick's older brother Jimmy stepped forward and asked a few men on the platform if one of them was Mr. Darcy, the farm owner. To this, one of the men nodded affirmatively and came forward. "Hello, I'm Jimmy Donato," Jimmy said, introducing himself. They shook hands. The farmer along with two of his workers led the families to three flatbed horse-drawn hay wagons which would transport them to the farm. This was a treat for all of the kids. On the other hand, the adults made the best of it and took it in stride.

After a short ride on a dusty road, they arrived at the Darcy homestead where fields of vegetables and orchards of fruit-bearing trees were in abundance. The lush land consisted of many acres of tomatoes, eggplants, green peppers, celery, and more. The orchards yielded early apples, sweet peaches, and cherries; the abundance truly was nature's blessing.

It was late in the afternoon when Mr. Darcy showed everyone around the immense barn where they would be staying. The well-kept structure included a second-floor loft. Directly outside were six stone fireplaces used for cooking. The fact that it was summer made sleeping in the barn not a problem and was in fact cooler than most houses. Mr. Darcy provided them with empty mattress covers which would be filled with sweet-smelling hay and would be softer and more comfortable than any manufactured mattress they were accustomed to. The mothers of the group were not that thrilled about it, but the children loved the idea of bedding down in the hay barn.

As for food, they had the entire farm at their disposal and would be well fortified with fresh eggs, milk, produce from the fields, and beautiful artesian spring water. Adding to their compensation for the coming weeks of work, each family would receive one hundred dollars, though the primary reason for going was to experience a pristine, natural setting.

That first evening, to the joy of the young people, supper was cooked over an open fire. The food seemed to taste many times better than that made at home. Huddled around the fire, the older boys told ghost stories that scared the daylights out of the younger kids. Before long, one family after another retired to the barn and its inviting aroma of fresh hay while a few of the older kids chose to sleep under the infinite display of stars.

After a blissful night of sleep, the area bristled with the energy of mothers making breakfast. The aroma of fried eggs enticed even the least hungry. When breakfast was finished, all the kids over twelve were led to the fields for their first day of work while the mothers stayed behind to do chores and supervise the younger children not allowed to work. Due to the large number of kids in the families, there were always four or five who were of age and able to harvest crops. Dominick's older brothers Jimmy, Tony, and Frank along with sister Rose left to labor in the fields while he and younger Carly remained with Carolina to help prepare lunch and do laundry. The latter was no easy task. Even under ordinary conditions back home, laundering was laborious using a washboard and Kirkman's borax soap. First, water was drawn from a spigot that filled a trough used by thirsty farm animals. Then Dominick and Carly returned with heavy bucketfuls that they poured into the outdoor wash tubs. It took most of the morning for Carolina to complete the arduous task even with the boys' help.

Noon quickly arrived as the older children returned from the fields to have lunch. It was a happy time, for everyone was gathered around outdoor tables eating and talking about their busy morning. After an hour, Dominick's working siblings went back to harvesting.

Carly and Dominick helped Carolina clean up after lunch and then she informed them that they were free to go and play but told them to be back in time for supper.

They boys met up with their good friend Red and two others, and they all decided to go to the nearby lake. They walked along the dusty road and spoke excitedly about fishing. But they soon realized that no one had a string for a line. Red finally came up with the clever idea of spearing the fish with a sharp stick. Along the way, the boys managed to pick up a few considerably straight branches.

When they arrived at the lake, Red took out a small folding pocket knife and proceeded to make sharp points on their makeshift spears. They kicked off their shoes, rolled their knickers higher, and walked into the cold, shallow water. The immediate cool sensation between their toes was exhilarating. They spread out along the shoreline and looked for fish. Suddenly, Carly shouted out, "Look! There's one!" Dominick and Red splashed through the water with their spears raised while the others discovered something swimming toward them. Red was the first to throw, and Dominick followed. Both missed by a country mile and had a hard time retrieving their spears. The other two boys were equally unsuccessful at their attempts.

The next half hour was spent tossing and retrieving, and

soon they all gave up the grand idea of harpooning fish and instead skipped flat rocks across the lake. They had more success with this. Someone inadvertently splashed another which quickly escalated into everyone having a water fight. The day was hot, and getting wet was delightful. The end result was getting soaked through. Finally, Dominick suggested they gather their shoes and begin the trek back. They hoped by the time they returned that the late afternoon sun beating down on them would dry their clothes and they would not get in trouble with their mothers.

On the way back to the farm, a snake slithered across the dusty road. Not to let the opportunity go by, the boys harassed the creature by poking it with their sticks, though the mission was quickly abandoned when they realized it could be poisonous and continued on.

Carolina was becoming concerned that Dominick and Carly had not yet returned. It was almost supper time, and her other children had already finished work for the day. She told Jimmy and Tony to go up the road to the lake and look for them. Both sons agreed and assured that they would find the others.

The two brothers wasted no time and walked briskly on the not-so-traveled road. They had not gone a quarter of a mile when they saw five figures up ahead. Tony waved, and one of them motioned back. Within a minute or so, they met up with the five bedraggled boys. "Hey, Dom, Carly...you look like you almost drowned. What happened?" Jimmy asked with a laugh.

"I slipped on a rock by the lake," Dominick responded.

"I guess you all slipped on the same rock," Tony interjected.

"Come on, let's go. Mom is worried," Jimmy said, adding, "But don't be nervous. Everything's okay."

Carolina was busy stirring a large pot on the fire when she glanced up and saw her sons walking toward her. She smiled with relief and said, "I was beginning to worry. I'm glad you're both safe." She wiped her hands on a towel and continued with a smile, "By the way, who washed your clothes? Apparently, they forgot to dry 'em." Everyone laughed at her whimsical remark.

A week later, on a lazy Sunday afternoon, Tony, Jimmy, and Frank—along with their older friends—hitched a ride on a farmer's wagon heading toward the Hudson River five miles away from the farm. The young men had gotten together for a cool dip and were all in good spirits, joking and talking. It was uncomfortably warm during the ride, but for the happy group, it went by almost unnoticed.

Within three quarters of an hour, the farmer stopped along the side of the road, and the anxious boys jumped off. He directed them to a path that led to the riverbank.

After a short walk, the city boys were at the tree-lined river's edge. Eagerly, they discarded their clothes, anticipating a refreshing swim. A few locals were gathered along the river and were amused by the zealous swimmers from the big city.

Soon, the young men plunged into the inviting current, diving beneath the surface then rising with seemingly unlimited energy. One by one, they took turns swinging from the heavy hemp rope tied to a large tree and jumping off into the rushing water.

When it was Jimmy's third turn on the rope, he took a few steps and swung out further, disappearing into the water. His brother Tony finally noticed his absence and dove in after him. Seconds later, he came up for air and still there was no sight of his brother. Those on the nearby riverbank realized the gravity of the situation and jumped in to help. One by one, they all resurfaced without success.

Unnoticed, further down the river, another stranger dove in. Half a minute later, the man broke the surface, pulling Jimmy behind him. Everyone else down shore finally realized what had happened and swam toward them to help. Once Jimmy was on shore, the stranger flipped him onto his stomach and started to revive him by putting his hands on the nearly-drowned youth and forcing water from his lungs. After a few attempts, Jimmy coughed up water and started to breathe again. Within a short time, he was breathing normally. His elated brothers and relieved bystanders cheered and could not thank the heroic man enough. It turned out that the Good Samaritan was a full-blooded native Mohawk who had fished and frequented the river all of his life.

When Jimmy had completely recovered, he explained to everyone that when he plunged into the water, he had apparently hit his head on a submerged log which rendered him unconscious.

On their way back to the farm, Tony and Frank asked Jimmy not to tell their mother or anyone else what had happened, and to blame the minor bruise on his forehead on a low-hanging branch. They figured it would only worry the rest of the family and would serve no purpose other than everyone being put under a watchful eye. Jimmy readily agreed.

Days went by much too rapidly as the families settled into laborious but nurturing farm life. Everyone psychologically prepared themselves for the inevitable departure from their bucolic interlude. The last day sadly arrived, and the families gathered their meager belongings for the return trip home. It had been a vacation for the younger children; however, the young adults and their mothers left with mixed feelings. Time spent on the farm was positive, but the difficult work did exact a toll and most looked forward to returning home to the neighborhood and the familiar routine of everyday life.

Once again, they all gathered in front of the large barn which had served them well as a temporary home, and as before, the families resembled a cluster of refugees waiting to be transported. The same three hay wagons that had brought them there arrived to take them to the railroad station. In less than an hour, they were all aboard the train. The massive engine hissed clouds of steam as it pulled away.

The three weeks spent on the farm made such an impact on all that it was nostalgically spoken of for years afterward.

Skipping School

The last days of August approached, and Dominick and his pals were nervous about the new school year. It loomed ominously ahead. They kept themselves busy and avoided thinking about the discipline, schedules, and teachers. The boys were ingenious in devising games and mischievous activities. They were intent not to squander what precious time that remained, but trouble lurked despite their pursuit of good times. Their hanging out at the corner and in front of the local businesses was becoming troublesome. More than one angry store owner with broom in hand would shoo them away. The card-playing little ruffians would just pick up and move to another storefront until they once again were told to leave. Adults in the neighborhood somehow survived the escapades of the idle, unruly boys.

On the last evening before returning to school, they gathered to play their street games one more time as free spirits. They engaged in serious games of Hide-n-Go-Seek, Kick the Can, and Johnny on the Pony. They became so engrossed that time ran away from them, and darkness enveloped the neighborhood. Soon, their mothers began calling from the windows, "Joey, it's getting late! Come on in!"

"Red, get inside before your father comes home!" said another.

"Dominick, come in now! I don't want your father to have to come and get you!" Carolina called. One by one the dejected boys left their haven in the street and reluctantly retreated to their homes, sending their last night of freedom.

The first week of school came and went as they resigned themselves to the inevitable strict schedule. Within a month, they went with the flow of attending school but soon developed a deep restlessness and resented the authority's upper hand.

Around that time, Red thought about skipping school and persuaded Dominick and the others to join him. It didn't take much arm bending to entice them, and soon a plan was hatched: the following morning, they would just pass by the school and walk a mile to a farm that raised chickens, pigs, and ducks. The place was ideal with its

45

numerous coops and sheds that could be used as a hide-out.

When the time came and the five friends did not show up for class, a truant officer was sent out to investigate their absence. Telephones were not common, so the officer would go directly to the child's home. It was an unenviable job, for most immigrants did not welcome strangers representing authority and they were met with total distrust.

That day, the truant officer patrolled the poorer sections where most of the local truants lived, including Dominick's neighborhood. Dressed in black, the tall and lanky Mr. Osborne was easily identifiable and stood out as a foreign intruder. "Mya son is notta here. He went to school. Thatsa where he is," was the response from most of the houses. Mr. Osborne knew the hardships of the families and was sympathetic. He did his job, nonetheless. After making his rounds, he scoured the neighborhood for any signs of the kids' whereabouts and went to their usual haunts. He asked business owners if they had seen the boys and was met with a wall of ignorance.

He searched vacant lots, railway yards, and where trolley cars were parked; feeling bold, he also inspected local pool rooms. As most times, Mr. Osborne's efforts ended fruitlessly because the cunning boys always appointed someone as a lookout which gave them an edge.

At the farm, Dominick and his friends had found a relatively safe refuge. They had figured out that it was far enough away and they would not be easily discovered. All had their school lunches made by their mothers so they would not go hungry. With the adjacent fields and wandering brook, it was an ideal location to focus on the most important thing: who would be the cowboys and who would be the Indians.

Hours went by as they enjoyed their forbidden freedom, and late afternoon was soon upon them. They knew it was a good half hour's walk back to the neighborhood, so they did not dawdle.

When they returned home, it was after their usual arrival time from school. When Dominick walked in the door with a guilty expression, his older brother Jimmy was sitting at the kitchen table with their mother Carolina. "Hey, Dom, did you stay after school today?" Jimmy asked immediately.

"Yeah, did some work for the teacher," Dominick answered, glancing downward.

"Oh, really? Gee, it must have been a group effort. A little while ago, I was talking to Red's mother and Bach's father, and they informed me that both of your friends were overdue in getting home," Jimmy stated. Carolina nodded, folding towels and remaining quiet, letting her eldest son handle the situation. Dominick's face flushed red with embarrassment.

"Yeah, we all had to help Miss Shantz with some special school project."

"Sure, Dom, I just bought the Brooklyn Bridge, too," chided Jimmy as he winked at their mother. "I heard that some kids from the neighborhood were skipping school. You don't know anything about *that*, do ya?"

"Nah. No one, I know," Dominick swore.

"You know, Pop would really be mad if he knew you did. You're lucky that he's at an Italian Society meeting tonight," Jimmy said firmly as Dominick remained quiet. And with that, the matter was put to rest and soon, everyone gathered around to eat an early supper.

The next morning, Dominick and his friends met at school and discussed how they were able to dodge the bullet with their parents. However, their teacher Miss Shantz, commented with tongue in cheek, "How quite *extraordinary* that a group of friends in my class were all sick on the same day. Well, I hope it wasn't contagious." She smirked.

The five friends reluctantly accepted their sequestered fate. Eventually, over the following weeks, the strict conditions once again began to wear on them. Soon, they were daydreaming about more freedom.

As before, Red was formulating another plan to escape school prison. This time, they picked Friday and hoped the weekend would take the edge off any disciplinary reprisals.

When the day arrived, they met on the corner as if on the way to school, but of course, walked past as they had done before. They were in such a good mood that they almost skipped toward their personal hideout at the farm. Discarding caution, they brazenly set out to have a great day.

Once there, they settled alongside an abandoned chicken coop on the perimeter of the land. The boys set up camp on the less visible side of the shabby structure. They collected eggs from the occupied coops to add to their bagged lunches. This was not an easy task, for the excitable roosting hens were not very cooperative with the boys' disruptive actions. Nevertheless, the truants felt safe enough to build a small fire to cook. They found a discarded pail and filled it halfway with water from the nearby brook. Since they had watched their mothers make soft-boiled eggs many times, they knew it did not require much cooking time. They set the pail on the fire and waited for it to boil as they devoured their lunches made from the previous night's leftovers. It seemed to take forever for the water to finally boil and the eggs to be cooked. They didn't have cups to put them in, so they stuck a pen knife through the eggshells, tilted their heads back and sucked the savory, golden liquid.

Once their appetites were satisfied, someone suggested they appoint a lookout as a precaution for the truant officer or the owner of the land who might come upon them unnoticed. They took turns every hour on the rooftop of the shed. From that vantage point, one could easily see half a mile in any direction making it easy to detect any intruder. The only drawback was the large opening which someone could easily fall through and into the old coop.

In time and a few observers later, it was Dominick's turn to be the lookout. He had only been there a few minutes when he saw the figure of a man approaching. He called out to the others, and Goose was the first to react and climb up to have a look. He was not the brightest of the bunch, but he was blessed with extraordinary eyesight and reaffirmed their worst fear: the tall, advancing figure was indeed the dreaded Mr. Osborne. "How did he know where to look?" Red questioned in disbelief, "Someone from the neighborhood must have ratted on us."

"Yeah, I know a couple of guys who would do that," added Bach.

"If we run for it now," Danny proposed, "he might be close enough to see us running in the field. I think I have an idea. Hey, Dominick, the hole in the roof, is it big enough for us to fit through?"

"No problem," Dominick answered.

"Are you thinkin' what I'm thinkin'?" Danny asked, looking at Red.

"That we should all drop through the hole and hide in the coop?" Red asked.

"Let's do it!" the others chimed in and started climbing up to the roof.

In a minute or two, all the boys were in the not-so-great-smelling shed while the long-legged Mr. Osborne came closer and closer. He stopped in front of the coop, removed his cap, and scratched his head, mumbling, "Didn't I see those boys or am I seeing things?" Inside, the boys stifled any response as they stared at his pant legs through the musty cracks. The truant officer decided to walk around the coop, and to his further bewilderment, came up with nothing and shook his head. He then glanced at the small opening where the chickens would enter and exit and realized the space could not have allowed the truants to squeeze through.

Inside, the nervous boys could hear Mr. Osborne's breathing as they remained silent and still. Once more, he circled the shed, and as before, fumed with frustration. Fed up, he turned and abruptly walked away.

Ten minutes later, Red was the first to pop his head through the opening in the roof and was overjoyed to see that no one was in sight. One by one, the boys exited their hiding place as each patted the other on the back and celebrated successfully outsmarting their arch enemy.

Newspaper Route

Some of the boys delivered newspapers to help their families and earn some spending money. For months, Dominick had asked his father if he would permit him to get his own paper route. Giuseppe was not in favor of his son delivering early in the morning and in all kinds of weather. Eventually, after months of pleading, he was finally worn down, and he gave Dominick his approval. The boy was ecstatic about earning some real money.

Within a couple of weeks, he had his own route delivering **The Brooklyn Daily Eagle**. The paper started him out with twenty-five copies, and when they saw he could easily handle it, increased his number to forty-five. Dominick found it easy to make the deliveries before school, and instead of walking, he balanced on one roller skate down the streets.

A news delivery truck dropped off bundles of tied papers at a candy and soda shop. They were protected from the weather inside a large, waist-high wood cabinet that stood outside the store. Dominick would reach into the sliding panel and put them into his two canvas sacks which crisscrossed his shoulders. During inclement weather, he sometimes arrived before the delivery truck and because of his small stature, was able to crawl inside the cabinet to stay dry. When ready and loaded up, he pushed himself off with his right foot then positioned it on top of his left skate.

He adapted well to this method of travel. In some situations, when he came to a steep hill, he would pump with much effort with his right foot to ascend to the top. His descent, on the other hand, was rewarding as he glided down and picked up speed. The unevenness of the streets were a problem, made worse by the manure left behind by horse-drawn wagons. Dominick had to gingerly dodge his way around to avoid hitting the clumps. There would be risk of injury if he failed to do so. In time, he became very proficient at weaving around such obstacles.

Dominick was exposed to a variety of personalities and economic stations along the route—from the poorest to the middle class to the very wealthy—and dealt well with the diversity of his patrons. The upper middle class and the old money rich fascinated him the most; it was intriguing and foreign to a boy who had very few material possessions. He skated past ornate iron fences and deftly tossed the folded paper onto long porches with heavy whickered furniture. Other homes were sometimes surrounded by high stone walls and impressive gates. More times than not, he never saw the privileged rich and most of his dealings were with servants and caretakers.

One early morning, as he was making his rounds, Dominick's eye caught something ahead in the middle of the street. When he approached, he realized it was an injured dog lying on its side apparently hit by a motorist who didn't care enough to stop. The animal was whimpering as Dominick crouched down. He recognized the German shepherd as belonging to the Thorntons a few houses away, and he knew he could not lift the animal by himself. Dominick quickly skated back to the Thornton residence and rang the bell. A maid opened the door, and he informed her of the dog's dire situation. She could see that he was very upset. While they talked in the doorway, the owner heard the commotion and came over. When Mr. Thornton realized what had happened, he and Dominick rushed back to the injured animal. The man knelt down, and as gently as possible, picked him up and hurried back to the house as Dominick followed. A closer inspection revealed that the dog's leg was broken. The owner turned to the boy and said, "Son, if you did not alert us when you did, I'm sure he would have been hit again by another motorist. I want to thank you very much for your heartfelt concern, young man."

"Oh, that's all right, Mr. Thornton. I didn't do that much," Dominick responded. "Well, I have to get back to my route and finish delivering. I hope the dog will be okay."

"What is your name, young man?"

"Dominick Donato, Sir."

"I'm going to call the publishers of the paper and tell them of your act of charity for a helpless animal. I will be forever grateful to you." Mr. Thornton and Dominick shook hands and then the boy returned to his route.

That evening at supper, he told his family what had occurred. Giuseppe was especially proud of his son, mostly for his magnanimous heart. The following morning, as usual, Dominick was arranging his papers for delivery when one of the newspapers he was folding fell open. He reached down to put the paper back in order when he noticed an article in the middle of the page: *Newspaper Delivery Boy Saves Dog.* Dominick couldn't believe his eyes but soon realized it was about him. He immediately bought three extra editions of the paper from the candy store and couldn't wait to get back home to show his family.

For days afterward, everyone, including his friends, were proud to have a celebrity among them. About a week later, Dominick saw Mr. Thornton in front of the his residence and noticed a small bundle under his arm. He was obviously waiting for him, and he waved to Dominick to join him on the front porch. "Hi, Mr. Thornton. By the way, thank you for calling the newspaper and having them print the article," he said with a gracious smile.

"My boy, you deserved it," he responded, "I've been informed that you like to read. So, I want you to have these six classics." Mr. Thornton handed him volumes by Dickens, James Fenamore Cooper, Robert Louis Stevenson, and Daniel DeFoe. Dominick gasped with great surprise and stared at the leather-bound books with appreciation. He had been completely caught off guard and did not know what to say but finally responded.

"No one has ever given me such a gift. Thank you so much! I don't know w-what to say..." Dominick exclaimed.

"You don't have to say anything, my boy. Please accept them." And with that, Dominick carefully placed them in his canvas sack and happily went on his way.

"You know, Dom, these classics can really inspire you and should help with your education if you let it," his brother Jimmy said, when he saw the beautiful gift of books from Mr. Thornton. For days afterward, Dominick had his head buried in one of the volumes. He was reluctant to acknowledge that they were becoming addictive. All of his brothers were also avid readers, so while Dominick read one book, they competed for the others.

Giuseppe was always a great advocate for education. As a young man in Italy, he attended a prestigious school of higher learning. Due to family circumstances, he had to abandon his dream of teaching. When he arrived in America, Giuseppe's scholastic credentials were not transferrable and not valid. Therefore, he had to accept positions below his actual level and potential. Regardless, he was selected over physicians and lawyers to be president of the Italian-American societies. Because he demonstrated eloquent speaking ability he became the official orator representing the greater New York area.

When it came to Dominick, Giuseppe realized he would be the one capable of having a professional career. At an early age, the boy gravitated to learning any new subject with relative ease. The only obstacles to his potential success would be the influence of his friends and the neighborhood. His interest in higher learning had to be nourished and required constant direction. This ultimately fell on the shoulders of his older brother Jimmy who made it his mission to see Dominick become a lawyer or doctor. Jimmy was dedicated to this objective, sometimes to Dominick's dismay. He became, according to Dominick, The Enforcer, who also encouraged him to be responsible, beginning with keeping his job as paper boy.

A few houses down from the Thorntons was another **Brooklyn Eagle** subscriber who also made an impression on young Dominick. The Baylor estate was a run-down mansion behind iron gates that still retained an aura of old wealth. It was occupied by an elderly woman and her odd, middle-aged bachelor son. Dominick very seldom saw any signs of life at the house, though the papers were picked up daily. Until one day in October when Dominick heard a voice beckon to him while he was delivering the paper. He turned around to respond. He saw a man pruning the lower branches of an apple tree in the small orchard just off the side garden. "Say, young man, can you please give me a hand? Hold this branch while I saw through it. I don't want it to split."

"Sure," Dominick said, going over to assist him. "You are Mr. Baylor, right?" The man nodded affirmatively as he

57

sawed the branch. A few more passes and the branch fell to the ground.

"Thank you for your help, young man," Mr. Baylor said.

"I always admire your apple trees when I walk by," Dominick commented. "I was wondering if it would be okay if my friend and I picked some apples this afternoon."

"Sure, take as many as you want. Most of them are likely to go uneaten, as my mother and I can only eat so many."

"Thanks so much, Mr. Baylor! See you later!" and with that, Dominick went on with his paper route.

Later that day, Dominick met up with his best friend Red and told him he had permission to pick apples. Red was all for it, and after school, they walked the five blocks to the fenced-in orchard. They went through the open gate, and Dominick took out one of his canvas sacks.

Each climbed a knobby tree and maneuvered limb to limb, shaking branches to loosen the crimson fruit. When enough fell, the boys scampered down and gathered the apples, stuffing them in the sack. All was fine until they heard Mr. Baylor's irate voice, "What are you boys doing?" Dominick looked at Red with confusion when the man came around the corner and angrily advanced toward them.

"B-but," Dominick stammered, "You said we could." The enraged man grabbed Red and held him in a tight grip. "Don't you remember? You told me this morning that it would be okay if I came back this afternoon to pick apples."

"I don't know what you are talking about, young man," he answered, dumping out the apples and dragging Red by the collar toward the house.

"Wait a minute!" Dominick yelled, following them. Once in the house, the half-crazed Mr. Baylor called the police and told them he would be bringing two thieves down to the station.

"Let me go!" Red demanded, but his nor Dominick's pleading did any good. Mr. Baylor maintained his hold on Red as he marched him out of the house and down the street with Dominick in tow. They had only gone one block when they met a police officer on his way to the Baylor home to investigate. Within seconds, the officer escorted them all to the precinct a block away. Once there, the boys stood in front of the sergeant's high desk. Still angry, Mr. Baylor insisted the youths be arrested for stealing and trespassing. "Why don't you tell me what happened and we'll go from there," the sergeant suggested to the nervous boys.

"He told me this morning I could bring a friend and pick some apples from his orchard," Dominick explained.

"Is that true?" the sergeant asked Baylor.

"Absolutely not!" the man spat back with a flushed face.

"Now look, someone is obviously not telling me the truth. Boys, I don't recall seeing you in this precinct before, but we've seen you many times, Mr. Baylor, mostly about nothing." The sergeant paused. "Let's get your parents down here and we'll try to settle this."

It wasn't long until the parents were summoned to the

station. Giuseppe had been home early from work and ready to leave for his society meeting. He arrived visibly upset, followed by Red's agitated mother a few minutes later. "Your boys are common thieves! How dare they come through my gate and take my apples!" Baylor ranted.

"Wait a minute," Red's mother interjected, but before she could finish the sentence, an additional police officer came over and whispered in the sergeant's ear before asking the parents to join him in another room. Other patrol officers were summoned to quiet the out-of-control Baylor.

After an anxious ten minutes, Red's mother and Dominick's father walked out of the room nodding their heads in agreement. "You can take the boys home now," the sergeant at the desk informed. "No charges will be filed." Dominick and Red sighed relief.

"What happened in there?" Dominick asked his father once they were outside the building.

"They told us it's not the first time Baylor did something like this. He has some sort of mental disorder that makes him forgetful," Giuseppe said, frustration and embarrassment making him walk at a faster pace.

"He's crazy!" Red yelled without restraint, the thought of the juicy apples still on his mind.

"Crazy or not, that man is not worth discussing. I am still not happy with you," Red's mother remarked to her son, dragging him by the ear and outdistancing Dominick and Giuseppe.

"Ma, I didn't do anything wrong! The guy's nutso!" Red

fought to no avail.

"That's for getting into trouble," she said, twisting his ear again. "Today and in the past. Do you think I have nothing better to do than keeping you outta jail? It's a disgrace!"

A few feet behind them, Dominick and Giuseppe had their own battle in progress. The boy walked ahead of his father to avoid a lecture, and Giuseppe tried in vain to catch up with his fast-moving son. This only made him angrier.

When they turned the corner at St. Mark's, Dominick broke into a sprint, leaving his father far behind. Within a few moments, he approached his house where Carolina was waiting anxiously for their return. When Dominick got close enough to his mother, he said, "Momma, Pop is really mad at me. It wasn't my fault."

"Here, my son, here's some money. Go across the street to the barber shop and get a haircut. Go, quickly." She handed him fifteen cents. "By the time you're finished getting your hair cut, your father will be out at the society meeting. When he gets home later tonight, he will be cooled off by then."

Dominick ran across the street to the barber and hastily sat down in a chair where he tried to hide behind a newspaper. Giuseppe arrived home and met Carolina on the steps. He couldn't help but notice his son through the window across the street. He put his hands on his hips and shook his head. He did not want to make a scene and refrained from going over and dragging Dominick home. Dominick was relieved to see his father finally keep going on his way to the meeting. *Whew, that was too close,* Dominick thought to himself.

Later that night, he told his mother he was going to bed earlier because he was tired. His mother agreed it would be a good idea. Three hours later, Dominick was still awake when he heard his father come home and decided that he better pretend to be asleep. As predicted, Giuseppe came into his room five minutes later and put his face close to his son's to determine if he was really asleep. Unconvinced but willing to let it go for now, he turned around and walked back into the kitchen.

Dominick heard coffee cups rattling and soft laughter between his parents. He was relieved for being saved by the bell but knew a lecture would surely come.

Surprisingly, the next morning and afternoon passed with no lecture. Dominick thought he was off the hook until shortly before supper when Giuseppe demanded to have a word with him. *Oh, Lord, I better make myself comfortable,* Dominick thought. *This is going to take a while.*

"What a disgrace it was to have to go to the police station because of you," he began, "The little offenses will lead to bigger and more serious offenses. You were not at fault this time, but you'd better change your choice of friends for your own good." Just then, Dominick's brother Frank opened the door. This was a great break for Dominick. Frank immediately sensed the tense atmosphere and froze when their father directed his attention to him. "Why are you hesitating? Close the door." Both boys knew it was a question not to be answered, for any answer would be wrong. Frank closed the door and quickly plopped down in a chair. It was a good decision, for the lecture went on for another forty-five minutes on the misadventures of both his sons—Frank with his gambling and reluctance to work and Dominick's escapades.

The doorbell rang, jolting all three of them. *Thank God,* Frank said to himself when they realized it was Mrs. DeVito from down the block. She came in wearing her usual sweater over a housecoat and her husband's wingtip shoes. "Good evening, Giuseppe. How are you?" she asked with a smile.

"Very well, Mrs. DeVito. How is everyone in the family?" Giuseppe replied, turning on a dime like Dr. Jekyll and Mr. Hyde. Dominick looked at Frank in amazement and relief. There was no way their father would continue the lecture in front of Mrs. DeVito. It was finally over.

Because of his natural curiosity, school was never difficult for Dominick, especially history which he liked best. Remembering his father's well-meaning castigation, he cultivated more self-discipline in class and his teachers became aware of his aptitude for learning. One in particular was a seventh grade teacher named Miss Morgan who had been teaching for twenty years and was admired by her peers. Over time, she witnessed Dominick's ability to absorb whatever he was exposed to and took a liking to the boy. She realized that he maintained a B average throughout the term without much effort. She pondered what he could achieve if he were in a more conducive environment. On report cards, she supported his efforts yet encouraged him to do even better because she knew his capacity.

Miss Morgan lived along Dominick's paper route and lived in a multi-turreted Victorian. He would see her sometimes outside on the front porch or in her small flower garden she tended to with great care. From the few snippets of conversation between them, Miss Morgan understood his intense desire to read and to someday travel to Europe. Their alliance became closer during the school term, and out of class, during their brief talks when he delivered her paper. She never failed to impart some guidance.

It was the last week of school when she asked to speak to him after class. Three o'clock rolled around, and Dominick waited for the rest of the students to file out. He thought he had done something wrong and was going to be reprimanded. "No, nothing like that, young man," Miss Morgan said with a smile and an expression that hinted of unexpected surprises. Dominick was relieved, but his curiosity was peaked. "I will be vacationing in Europe for six weeks this summer."

"Ah, shucks. That's great!"

"Dominick, from our talks this past year, I have come to understand how important a trip like that would mean to a boy such as you. If you still have a desire to travel, I am presenting this opportunity to you and your parents to consider. You are a very intelligent young man and could benefit greatly from European culture," she explained, leaving Dominick speechless for a few seconds before he answered.

"Are you serious?"

"Very serious, Dominick."

"I'd love to!" he blurted out without a minute's thought about the matter.

"Please inform your parents I would pay for everything."

"This is too good to be true, Miss Morgan. A-are you sure?"

"Yes, by all means. I will speak to your parents if this is something you want to do."

"I'd do anything to go!" he exclaimed with wide-eyed eagerness.

"Very well, then. Talk it over with your parents and we shall go from there." Miss Morgan smiled, equally as enthused.

It wasn't long until Dominick flew down the school steps and raced home. His mother thought something dreadful had happened when he barreled breathlessly through the kitchen. His sister Rose had stopped slicing vegetables and waited expectantly for an explanation of such an entrance. "Momma, you're not going to believe what Miss Morgan asked me today," Dominick began to explain, putting both hands on his mother's shoulders.

"All right, Dominick, just catch your breath so I can understand what you are about to tell me," Carolina said, putting her dish towel on the counter. Dominick paused to regain his composure and continued.

"She wants me to go with her on a summer trip to

Europe, all expenses paid! Isn't that great?"

"Are the rest of the kids going?" she asked, confused.

"No, just me!" Dominick grinned.

"Dominico, I do not like this."

"Me, neither," Rose added, going back to peeling onions. It wasn't long until the boy's elation completely dissipated, and he stood there disappointed.

"But wait, Momma!"

"When your Papa comes home, we'll talk again," Carolina said ominously. He knew right then and there that his chances of going were nil, for his mother had a great influence on his father's decisions.

Within the hour, Giuseppe walked through the door and placed the daily paper on the table. He immediately detected an unsettled atmosphere and asked his wife, "Carolina, what's wrong? Why is Dominick sulking so?"

"We must talk over something *importante*," she whispered.

"Well, let's do it now before we all sit down to eat," he suggested, and without hesitation, Carolina began to explain about Miss Morgan's offer to Dominick. Giuseppe reacted calmly and pensively and did not say anything until Carolina finished. Dominick, on the other side of the table, wanted to jump into the conversation but didn't dare. Giuseppe took many moments of silent contemplation to weigh the situation. Dominick held his breath, waiting what seemed forever. Giuseppe finally spoke.

"Dominico, this is a very generous offer and chance of a lifetime," he began, "but it is a long length of time to be away from us and in foreign lands. My main concern, my son, is your safety. We live in an unstable, harsh world. God forbid, some unforeseen danger should arise and take you from us. I would never forgive myself for putting you in such a precarious situation. So, even though it sounds wonderful, I cannot put you in a stranger's custody. I am sorry." He paused, and Dominick slumped in his chair. "Miss Morgan is probably a fine person, but your mother and I do not know her. We cannot let you go."

"But!" Dominick tried to interject.

"When you are older, you will be able to travel and make a similar trip. You will also understand why our answer must be no," he concluded.

Dominick was devastated and spent the rest of the evening brooding. He went to bed earlier that night, and everyone was more somber than usual.

The next morning he hardly ate any breakfast and left quietly for school. Before class began, he told Miss Morgan that he was not able to go, and his parents' decision was firm. "Maybe I can speak to them," she suggested with a glimmer of hope.

"I don't think that would be a good idea," he advised.

"Well, I have no choice other than to honor their decision." Miss Morgan put her hand on his shoulder with assurance and said goodbye for the summer.

After the school year officially ended, Miss Morgan embarked on her vacation but took time once a week to send Dominick a postcard describing her latest destination. In the weeks to come, he looked forward to receiving a new, colorful foreign postcard and dreamed of someday venturing there.

However, to Dominick's dismay, when the new school year began in September, he saw a definite change in Miss Morgan's attitude toward him. Her indifference reached such a level that he felt invisible. It was a lesson in human nature that would remain with him for a long time.

Money in the Shoe & the Runaway Horse

Dominick's older brothers Tony and Frank always had a constant rivalry between them, and their personalities were starkly different. Tony, older and bigger of the two, was laid back and accepted life's realities. Frank, on the other hand, was very dynamic and there was nothing he believed he could not do if he put his mind to it. Tony always worked at some physical, demanding job and was a loyal and strong young man. Frank was sly at making money, and he was first in line whenever a get-rich-quick scheme presented itself. If he wasn't playing cards or shooting dice, he was busy playing numbers. Tony would give their parents a portion of his pay and would conceal the remainder of the money in an old pair of rarely-used shoes. He figured the five dollar bill would be safe, but because the two brothers shared the same bedroom, each knew the other's habits and hiding places.

One time, Tony needed a new belt and went to his stash to get some money. He was angered and surprised to find the five dollar bill missing. The only other person who would have had knowledge of his hiding place was of course, his smart aleck brother Frank. He found his mother in the kitchen and asked where his brother might be and was informed that Frank had gone out to eat with his friends. Tony had a good idea where his gallivanting brother would go.

He quickly headed to the end of St. Mark's Ave. and as he turned the corner, saw Frank walking away with two of his buddies. Tony immediately increased his pace until he was right behind his unsuspecting brother. He tapped Frank on the shoulder, and he turned around with surprise. "Hey, Tony, how are ya doin'?" Frank asked, trying to appear nonchalant.

"I'm doin' fine," commented Tony, "I think you have something that belongs to me."

"What are you talkin' about?" he snapped back, insulted.

"You know what I'm talkin' about."

"No, I don't, and you can search me if you don't believe me." Frank spread his arms innocently, but his face was red as a beet. One of his friends chuckled under his breath but tried to keep a straight face.

"Okay, I think I will. Pull your pockets inside out," Tony demanded. After Frank did what he asked, his pockets proved to be empty. "Okay, nothing there," Tony commented with sarcasm and then continued, "Now take off your shoes." With tongue in cheek, Frank complied by removing his left shoe. Again, nothing. He went a step further and removed his sock.

"See, Tony? Nothin'. I don't suppose you would want me to waste your time by taking my other shoe off." Tony scratched his head in mock thought.

"You probably don't have what I thought you had, but for the hell of it, take off your other shoe, too." Frank sighed but bent over to make the motion of taking off his remaining shoe then suddenly burst into a run leaving his friends in shock. He ran down the street with one shoe on and his irate brother sprinting behind. After three blocks, Tony was finally closing in on Frank right in front of the building where their father worked. As he did every day at lunch time, Giuseppe was seated in front of a second-story window facing the street. A blurred object caught his eye, and he looked down at the sidewalk to see his son Frank running like a bat out of Hell. "Francesco, what is this?" Giuseppe yelled out the window.

"Pop, no time to talk! See ya later!" Frank answered breathlessly. Within seconds, Giuseppe saw Tony running in pursuit. He looked up at his bewildered father.

"Pop, can't stop. I have to catch him!" Giuseppe shook his head as his sons disappeared from sight.

Frank was frantic as Tony gained on him, and he lost his balance when he looked over his shoulder. He careened into an unfortunate peddler, sending his goods into the air. The stunned man looked on as Frank fell onto the sidewalk. Within a second, Tony was on top of his brother pulling off his other shoe. Once he found the five dollar bill, he left Frank to explain himself to the peddler.

That night at supper, Giuseppe—ashamed of his sons' actions—read the riot act to both of them and called them a disgrace. Because of Frank and Tony, the rest of the family had to bear witness to the tirade that went on for an hour.

It would take a few days for the tension to dissipate. Finally, a calmer atmosphere prevailed as things returned to normal.

Later that week, Dominick and his friends sat on the sidewalk beneath the shade of a tree and discussed the latest Tom Mix movie playing at the local theater. Meanwhile, at the end of the block near the corner, Rocco the vegetable peddler had just turned his wagon from Troy Avenue onto St. Mark's. As soon as he appeared, the local women emerged in the effort to be first to select the best and ripest of the produce. Rocco tried to maintain politeness to his customers, but it was very difficult to do so with a half dozen women circling and asking, "How mucha? Are they fresh and sweet?" There was always some aggressive customer, who without hesitation handled the produce with disregard. Somehow, the amiable and good-hearted Rocco kept his composure. On this particular day, he had brought along his five-year-old son who was sitting up front on the wagon. The boy was a little intimidated by the over-zealous and boisterous women. Dominick and his friends were also distracted by the commotion around the produce. Red commented, "Poor Rocco, he is a good guy. I don't know how he doesn't lose his temper."

"I know what you mean. Our mothers can be very tough to deal with," added Dominick. The boys resumed playing cards. Bach, on the other side of Red, glanced up and saw Biff, the terror of the neighborhood. The dog was a large boxer mix with the angriest attitude around. He was so feared that the locals would cross to the other side of the street when they saw him. All of the attempts made by dog catchers had been unsuccessful, for he was just too sly and vicious. The boys instantly stiffened as Biff strolled by them. Fortunately, he was focused on going somewhere and did not even look in their direction. They breathed a sigh of relief and returned to their card game. Rocco and the haggling customers were unaware of the potential danger approaching them. Biff headed toward the loud throng and paused on the perimeter as if deciding what to do next. Within seconds, he put his head down and charged through without warning. A frightened woman screamed when he grabbed hold of the hem of her long skirt. He growled and shook his head viciously. Rocco's horse reared up. The peddler quickly remembered that his son was still in the front seat of the wagon but could not react in time. The spooked horse bounded down the street with the petrified crying boy. Dominick, Red, and Bach dropped their cards when they saw the runaway horse and wagon. "You stay here on this side of the street," Red said to Dominick, "I'll go on the other side of the street. Do what I do. Quick, let's go!" Red ran across and waited until the excited horse ran in their direction. Before the horse went by, Red moved closer to the center of the street in anticipation. The second before he was about to pass, Red leapt up and grabbed the horse's bit and hung on. Dominick dashed out and did the same from the other side as Bach looked on wide-eyed. With the weight of both boys pulling down on his bit, the frantic horse began to slow down and was soon brought to a halt.

Red looked at Dominick and said with relief, "We did it, buddy, we did it!" Dominick continued to hold onto the horse, calming him with gentle strokes on the nose as Red checked to see if Rocco's little boy was not injured. The boy was crying and scared but not hurt. Rocco caught up with them and was relieved to see his son was not harmed. He then embraced Red and Dominick, expressing deep gratitude. "You are both guardian angels who came to save my son," he said with emotion. A small crowd of onlookers had gathered and were now cheering. They were proud of the two local boys. Rocco and his fortunate son slowly continued on their way, and Dominick and Red started to walk back to meet Bach. Red noticed his friend limping and said, "Did you get hurt?" Dominick nodded. "Why didn't you say somethin'?"

"It's not that bad." The two boys sat on the curb, and Dominick removed his shoe and blood-soaked sock to inspect the damage. A closer look revealed his toe nail had been ripped off.

"Oh, no" Red said when he saw his friend's foot. "How

the heck did that happen?"

"Well, when I was trying to slow the horse down, I got too close and his hoof came down before I could get out of the way."

"That must hurt like Hell."

"Believe it or not, it only hurt when it happened. Don't worry." And with that, Red helped Dominick hobble back home.

Despite Dominick's injury, the boys' heroic actions that day were the focus of attention and were the talk of the neighborhood for a few weeks. Every time Rocco appeared on the street with his produce wagon, he would look for the boys and give them sweet plums or succulent, ripe peaches.

As for Dominick's toe, things were a bit difficult, for he had to walk with a cut-out shoe for a month. It eventually healed, and he returned to his paper route and mischief.

Boys Home

Surrounded by Prospect Pl.; Troy, St. Mark's, and Albany, the imposing edifice St. John's Home for boys had been built in the mid-1800s and evoked a medieval air. The Home's dominating presence loomed over the nearby crowded streets; with its entranceways and inner courtyards paved with heavy cobblestone, it had the appearance of a modern day fortress. It was run by the Sisters and Brothers of St. Joseph and at one time, housed up to a thousand orphaned boys.

Dominick and his friends would often play baseball on St. Mark's near Troy where there was less bustle, but more times than not, the ball would inadvertently fly over St. John's wall. Retrieving it was an ordeal, for the boys on the other side relished the prospect and waited for it to happen. The boys enjoyed not giving the ball back, and Dominick and his friends would have to resort to appealing to the nuns, but most times, it went without success. The St. John's boys pledged ignorance of ever seeing the ball when they were challenged by their authorities. It was infuriating for Dominick and the other neighborhood boys because of financial allowances, the school did not always promise the purchase of new baseballs. To add to the frustration, the St. John's boys would routinely climb the wall and brazenly walk along the rim for the thrill of taunting passersby. They thought nothing of throwing stones at their unfortunate victims below. Women and the elderly were not spared from their abuse, and young women in particular were the targets of their verbal assaults. Despite efforts to halt the incorrigible behavior, local people had learned to put up with it for years.

The rivalry between the orphans and the neighborhood boys was exceptionally intense. One hot afternoon, as Dominick and his buddies played cards in the cool shadows beneath the stone wall, above them, an unseen number of troublemakers quietly schemed to launch a barrage of projectiles. Out of the blue, a shower of debris rained down on the unsuspecting kids below.

Bach was able to dodge out of the way. Red was not as fortunate and was hit by a large rock that glanced off his shoulder. Dominick raised his arm and deflected a piece of iron pipe from hitting him in the face. Joey, on the other hand, turned his head away but had been struck on the forehead by an empty pop bottle, and blood instantly trickled down his face. The ambushed boys moved out of range of the projectiles as they continued to rain down.

Bach and Dominick wanted Joey's bleeding head to be

tended to and swiftly escorted him home. It was obvious that the injury required stitches. Red and the others tried to retaliate by tossing debris back over the wall where it came from, but it was ineffective. "This is not over!" Red shouted, "We'll be back soon, so enjoy yourselves! See ya!"

Joey was taken to St. Mary's Hospital, but the wound required only a few stitches. The tending doctor said he was fortunate to not have been hit in the eye and he could have been blinded. The following few days in the neighborhood were quite calm for a change. The boys who had been hurt by the hooligans of St. John's were busy devising a plan for their revenge. They decided that early Saturday morning would be the ideal time for their counterattack because the orphanage boys always played sports at 9. a.m. It was their daily routine, and it never wavered.

The night before they unfolded their plan, Dominick and his friends acquired a ladder and silently climbed to the top of St. John's wall to place what they would hurl down the following morning.

Dominick left the house earlier than usual and told his parents he would be finishing his paper route by 8:45 a.m. because he and his friends had something to do. After fulfilling his paper deliveries just in time, Dominick dashed around the corner of St. Mark's and Troy and breathed a sigh of relief to see his friends gathered at the wall with ladder in hand. There stood Red, Goose, Bach, Danny, and two other boys named Albert and Lou who had also experienced serious run-ins with the wild boys of St.

John's. They positioned the ladder on even ground and secured it well.

Red was up first and peeked over the top to find the delinquents predictably playing ball. He scanned the bunch to find the ones responsible for the injuries inflicted upon his friends. He soon realized they were directly beneath him sitting with their backs against the wall. One by one, each of the neighborhood boys scampered up the ladder and took a place at the top of the wall. Other St. John's boys in the courtyard below noticed the intruders above, yet the older boys who had participated in the assault a few days prior were still not aware of what was about to happen. Taking advantage of this, the righteous avengers started to throw down heavy rocks and bottles on the culprits' heads. Startled and enraged, they ran for cover while being hit from almost every angle. The St. John's perpetrators who were once so brave were screaming and running for help. Red, Dominick, and the others swiftly descended the ladder when they saw they had inflicted enough damage. They disappeared into the safety of the neighborhood, satisfied that they had settled the score, at least for the time being.

Winter Streets

It was a week after Thanksgiving, and the predominately Italian and Irish students were busy preparing for the anticipated Christmas season. The children made posters of snowmen and bundled-up figures ice skating and sledding on wintry hillsides. Boys and girls were chosen for parts in the colorful nativity play dramatizing the birth of Jesus. The interval between holidays was an infectiously hopeful time. Even the most negative and contrary individual could not help but be more agreeable. Due to the happy atmosphere, even Dominick and his friend Red were inspired enough to look forward to going to school. The mornings were colder, and frost collected on anything made of glass or metal. Dominick would leave his house in the early hours to deliver his newspapers and bristle from the cold on his way to the candy store. As usual, he would sort through the tied bundles, rearranging them for delivery. After his canvas sacks were loaded, he pushed off on his single skate, his wool scarf flowing behind and his cap pulled down over his ears. His brown corduroy knickers and high knee socks were the common attire for most boys, and thirteen-year-old Dominick was no exception. After delivering papers, he met up with his friends on the way to school and talked of things they were going to do that day.

One day during school hours, the temperature dropped considerably. Dominick had been staring out the window when he saw the first snowflakes of the season. His classmates soon realized it was snowing, and they all let out a happy cheer. Their teacher was amused but tried to get the boisterous, excited children under control. Everyone couldn't wait to play in the first snow.

Once dismissed, Dominick, Bach, and Red were already discussing the snow forts and igloos they would build. A few inches had already fallen when the boys made snowballs to bombard the girls and rival boys.

They would have fun, but as they made their way home along St. Mark's and saw their homes, they realized their fun would be short lived. Once they were inside, their mothers would demand homework to be done and to sit down to an early supper. There was no way they would be allowed out on a school night and had to accept the reality.

After supper, their noses were pressed against the windows as they watched the snow come down. All they could do was fantasize about being outside and reveling in the snow.

The storm continued throughout the night, and by morning the accumulation was eight inches deep. Though happy to see the snow, Dominick and the other neighborhood kids were disappointed that school remained open and they had to trek to school.

To the children's delight, the snow intensified through the morning hours. Another six inches had fallen by lunchtime, and someone came into the classroom and whispered in the teacher's ear. She nodded and then announced with a smile, "Gather your things. You are dismissed for the day." A loud cheer instantly erupted as the kids grabbed their belongings and raced outside. It was Friday, and they didn't have to return until Monday. Snow on Friday and all weekend to play in it was considered hitting the jackpot.

Snow fell all that day and into the night, and it was too deep for anyone to be out. The children and their parents went to sleep not knowing when the storm would come to an end. The wind howled as it whipped the snow into deep drifts. This did not seem to interfere with the children's sleeping; on the other hand, the adults had a much harder time hoping their families would be safe.

The next morning revealed a vivid blue sky, and the sun glistened brightly on the pristine, deep snow. The crystalline granules reflected a spectrum of sparkling colors. Dominick and his brothers quickly devoured breakfast as each wanted to be the first to emerge from the doorway and set foot on the pure, unbroken snow. The competition ended when Dominick and older brother Tony exited simultaneously. Tony allowed his younger brother to go ahead of him with a smile. Red, across the street, had already begun a path through the almost two feet of white. Portions of the street were hidden by high drifts that would not be removed for days.

The stinging, crisp air was invigorating for Dominick as he devoted his energy to digging a path that would connect with Red's across the way. Soon the entire neighborhood was alive with people clearing streets and sidewalks. By noon, the road was honeycombed with connecting paths, although it was still impossible for trucks or wagons to pass. The surrounding neighborhoods were also isolated from the rest of the borough.

In the latter part of the afternoon, the local boys met with each other and began constructing two snow forts, each on opposite sides of the street. The boys built them equally strong like their older brothers had advised, and they were all grateful for the tips. Once they were completed, the task of making dozens of snowballs came next, then finally, deciding which fort each group of boys would claim. This was usually the most contentious part. Each side of course, wanted the best and most accurate snowball throwers.

Finally settling on the members of the teams, the boys split up and went to their respective forts. On the given signal, both sides pelted each other, hiding and ducking out of the path of hurling snowballs. Neither side seemed to be gaining advantage, and it appeared that a stalemate would probably be inevitable. Then without any anticipation, someone yelled, "Charge!" as one team left the protection of their fort to attack the other. Without hesitation, the opposition responded with a vigorous counterattack. They clashed in the center of the street, throwing as many snowballs they could carry. Because they were all at such close range, everyone hit their intended target, and within no time at all, they ran out of ammunition and laughed at the situation.

The fun continued once they made new snowballs as the afternoon light waned, but regretfully, one by one, the boys were called in for supper. They hoped they would be allowed to go outside again after eating as they watched the full moon rise early and reflect brightly off the pristine snow. It was a Saturday night, and that alone tipped the scales in their favor. To their delight, permission was granted. Dominick asked his father if he could borrow the snow shovel, for he and Red had planned on clearing some of the neighbor's sidewalks and steps. Earlier in the day, some older people agreed to pay them for their work.

The snowy, moonlit night was a beautiful setting as the two friends went from house to house clearing walkways. The people appreciated their hard work. The hours flew by unnoticed as Dominick and Red made their way down the block. Had it not been for one of the people who hired them reminding them of the time, they would have never known it was almost ten o'clock. The two boys finished up with their last customer and slung their shovels on top of their shoulders and headed home. Dominick and Red were jubilant about earning almost nine dollars, which they divided equally.

When they arrived in front of their homes, Red said, "I hope you don't get in trouble for being out late. Good luck. See ya tomorrow."

"I hope not," Dominick glanced over his shoulder and shook his head. "You, too. See ya." Dominick placed the shovel outside the door and then hesitated before going in, for he did not know what to expect from his parents. Finally, he sheepishly opened the door to find his father puffing on his pipe and his mother sipping coffee. Giuseppe addressed Carolina, "Who said our son got lost?"

"I'm sorry. I lost the track of time. Red and I were so busy shoveling snow, we just forgot," Dominick answered. Giuseppe winked at his wife.

"I didn't realize we had such a big business man for a son." Carolina smiled and clasped her hands on the kitchen table. "My son, I'll let this go because it is a magnificent winter night and the weekend. Though, next time, try to get home a little earlier."

"Thanks, Pop. I will." Dominick breathed a sigh of relief and then brightened. "But the good news is that we each made four dollars and thirty-five cents!" Giuseppe took the pipe from his mouth with surprise. "And Pop, I want to give you three dollars for the family." Giuseppe was impressed by his son's generosity, and his eyes filled with emotion.

"My son, you don't have to. You worked hard for that money."

"No, Pop. Please, let me do this. I want to help."

"Alright, Dominick, I know it's coming from your heart. Grazie, thank you. You can give the money to your mother."

Dominick went over to his mother and gently placed the dollar bills in her apron pocket. Carolina kissed her son on the forehead and said, "We are blessed to have such a good boy. Mil grazie."

That night, Dominick was gracious and fell asleep knowing he was able to help the people he loved.

The following few days, the temperature plummeted to near-zero. The streets had been cleared enough so trucks and wagons could resume delivery of much needed food and coal, but they were covered with two inches of hard, hazardous ice and made traveling slow and treacherous. It was a common scene to see a horse and sleigh transporting people and goods. The sleighs seemed to manage these conditions best. Almost every day, heavy-laden trucks would get stuck on the thick mantle of slick ice and other trucks would have to come to their aid with ropes and pulleys. There were occasions when it was so slick that rescue vehicles also bogged down with their tires spinning helplessly. In this situation, teams of horses were called upon to pull the trucks out of the snow and ice. A sad, common occurrence was to see a horse pulling a wagon collapse on the ice. Usually, the poor animal's numerous attempts failed, and the injured horse could not be hoisted upright, whereupon his owner summoned a policeman to put the suffering animal out of misery. Adults along with children were witness to this troubling, stark reality.

The boys used the extreme cold to their advantage and took command of a section of sidewalk that was least traveled where they intended to make a "serious" sliding pond. Dominick, Red, Bach, and the others each went home to fetch buckets of water, and when they returned, poured the water on the frozen sidewalk. Their goal was to create an icy area four feet wide by twenty-five feet in length. After a few trips of hauling water, the slide was ready. The severe temperature caused the water to freeze on contact and worked out great. Soon the ice was extended to the desired length. Their leather-soled shoes and boots slid perfectly over the surface. Each boy was anxious for his turn to glide on the slick, hard ice, and one by one, they gave themselves a running start to the slippery slide. With outstretched arms, they desperately tried to maintain their balance as they swiftly skimmed along. This simple act of fun gave them great joy, and it soon became infectious as older boys joined in. Young adult passersby also could not hold back from giving it a try. People formed a line and waited their turn on the ice, and happy sounds of folks enjoying the moment filled the air. To the boys' delight, their sliding pond was a bigger success than they could have anticipated.

It remained brutally cold, and the conditions of the slide were easily maintained and even extended to almost thirty-five feet. Throughout the rest of the week, it was the boys' main source of entertainment while schools remained closed due to the harsh conditions of the roads.

One drawback of winter was that it hindered the boys from playing cards outside on the sidewalks, but one day Bach had a good idea. "Since trolley cars have electric heaters, why don't we go to the trolley depot?" The cars that were in use were kept on the perimeter of the lot to go in and out; the ones not in use were usually buried in the center of the depot and never moved. "All we have to do is sneak in, go in the middle of the parked trolleys and pull the pole up to the live wire. That will start the electric heater in the car. It's perfect!"

"Boy, why didn't I think of that?" praised Dominick.

"Yeah, it sounds great!" added Red.

"Let's do it!" Goose agreed with enthusiasm. And so, on that cold, dreary Saturday afternoon the boys headed out to the depot. They walked briskly, for there was a constant biting wind that plagued them the entire five blocks. It was a relief to arrive at the yard where the wind was blocked by the many parked trolleys. The open depot had a large roof supported by looming telephone poles, and crisscrossing electric wires formed an aerial network which supplied the power to the cars.

The boys made their way among the stationary cars but were on the lookout for the yardman whose job was to prevent vandalism. There were so many cars that he usually only made a cursory inspection by scanning the outer circle of trolleys. This left the center cars safe from his eyes; the fact that he remained in his heated booth on the outer edge added to the boys' chances of not being discovered. With this in mind, they weaved through the cars until they chose one in the center and went to the rear. There they hoisted the pole to the live wire; the car immediately responded with a humming vibration. They pushed a lever which provided heat and light.

The boys spent the next three and a half hours happily playing cards and talking, but the time to get back home came too quickly. They all agreed it would be better not to anger their mothers and arrive home in time for dinner. With great reluctance, the boys left their warm confines that had been an ideal secret haven on a cold winter day.

Dominick caught the aromas of his mother's tomato sauce as he approached home, and snowflakes began to fall once again and catch the dim light of the street lamps flickering on one by one. He momentarily realized how fortunate he was to have a family and a warm house to go home to. Upon opening the door, he saw his brothers Carl and Tony lingering in the kitchen to the objections of both his mother and his sister Rose. His brother Jimmy and their father were already seated at the table and looking at the daily newspapers and commenting on the current events. Dominick washed up and took a seat between Carl and Tony as their mother and sister Rose brought the food to the table before sitting down. Giuseppe, a little disgruntled, pulled out his pocket watch and stated, "There seems to be someone missing at the table."

"Pop, Frank told me he would be late for supper. He had something important to do," Tony said, covering for his brother.

"Well, we all can't wait," Giuseppe decided, adding, "Let's thank God for this food He has provided and hope others are doing the same. Mangia."

Everyone around the table was soon busy eating and chattering about the day's events. All in all, each person showed a genuine interest in the experiences of the others, and their warmth and caring were undeniable.

Supper was almost finished when Giuseppe shook his head. "I wonder when our missing son will make an appearance. He must be some important big shot."

"Ah, Pop," Jimmy interjected, "Frank is Frank. Always involved in some kind of deal. He should have a secretary so we could make an appointment with him."

Twenty minutes later when the table was just about cleared, in walked the Prodigal Son. "Mom, Pop...sorry," Frank apologized, "I couldn't break away."

"Hey, Frank, that's selfish. You're making double work for Mom, and you're upsetting Pop," Jimmy chided.

"No, it is okay," their mother said, "I don't mind. Just sit down and eat." Their father and Jimmy shook their heads with frustration.

"Yeah, brother, you got away with it again. You're just impossible," Jimmy criticized.

"Jimmy, enough. Let Frank eat," Carolina interrupted.

When things settled down later that evening and Carolina cleaned up the kitchen, Dominick asked her to tell him and his brother Carl about their grandfather's exploits. Carolina agreed, and on that winter night, they all gathered around the cozy warmth of the coal stove. Carolina told her sons about her father and his youthful adventures in the mountains of Calabria. The boys, especially Dominick, were enthralled by the exciting stories of their grandfather Antonio and his times.

When it came time for bed, Dominick fantasized about being back in 1860s Italy bounding across the countryside in the Cavalry with his grandfather.

Three blocks from St. Mark's Ave. was an underdeveloped area called Murphy's Hill. It was a large, open space half a block wide and within its center was a forty foot hill, the highest point within half a mile. Because of its height, children and young adults would flock to the spot to sleigh ride. It was a popular place during the snowy months of the winter, the steepness of the hill providing an exhilarating ride.

Dominick, Red, Bach, Goose, and Joey decided to go sledding, but there was one small glitch: they only had two old sleds among them. It wasn't long until conniving Red suggested they divert their trek to the hill by first walking through a wealthy neighborhood where they could borrow a few sleds left on the front porches. "We'll borrow 'em for a while and then bring 'em back after we're done," he said, the rest of the gang eventually going along with it.

Fortunately for the boys, the residents were not home, and it was relatively easy to confiscate two more sleds. When they arrived at Murphy's Hill, there were already two dozen others taking advantage of the slick conditions. Everyone was having fun, their screams of delight piercing the air. Dominick and his friends climbed to the crest of the hill and marveled at the three hundred foot run which veered left and ended in a small knoll. To the right, the straightaway dangerously curved, crossing a snow-covered street before continuing for another hundred yards before ending in a wooded area.

Most of the boys on the hill chose to use the safer run on the left side and were satisfied with it. The so-called big boys wanted more adventure and picked the longer and more dangerous run on the right. Goose, Bach, and Joey decided to take their turns on the left. After the run, they walked back, dragging their sleds to the top, while Dominick and Red waited for them to return so they could take their turn. Red held his sled and asked, "Dom, are you game to take the tougher run?"

"Well, I don't know," Dominick said, mulling it over and a little unsure. "I never went down that side before."

"Don't worry. I did it last winter, and it was fine."

"Oh, alright," Dominick said, "since you've already been on it, I'll follow you down." With that, Red took a few steps back and with a running start, dove onto the sled belly down. A second later, Dominick followed closely behind as the steel runners slid over the ice-crusted snow. Red glided down smoothly and soon approached the bottom. He followed the curve and banked to the right. He picked up more speed as the course straightened and his sled quickly flew toward the street ahead. Red, from his right side, caught a glimpse of a fast-moving black car on a collision course. At that point, there was no stopping; Red had to cross the road. In a split second, within a hair's breadth, he sailed in front of the car and safely reached the other side. Right behind him was Dominick, and he realized it was impossible to swerve and avoid the car. He suddenly decided to roll off the speeding sled, tumbling into a snowbank as the sled continued on and broke into pieces against the car's rear tire. The frantic driver immediately slammed on the brakes and skid to a stop. He got out and ran over to the demolished sled, not realizing that Dominick had rolled out of harm's way. When the man set eyes on him, Dominick was busy dusting snow off his clothes. "Son, I hope you are not hurt," the driver said with concern.

"Believe it or not, Sir, I'm okay."

"I'm so relieved that you are. Thank God. I'm sorry your sled didn't make out so good."

"Don't worry about it, Sir," Dominick said, "it was my fault. I shouldn't have tried to go across the street."

Red trudged back to the scene and was very glad to see his friend uninjured but readily took the blame for what had just happened. It was his idea to take the more dangerous route, and he apologized to Dominick. "Look, Red, I'm not a baby. I didn't have to follow you if I didn't want to. Come on, let's go." Dominick picked up the pieces of the sled, and he and Red walked back up the hill to join the others.

When their friends heard what had happened, they all sighed relief that no one else took the dangerous route down. To lighten things up, Goose told them what had happened to him. He had borrowed his brother's sled, which had been their father's and close to fifty years old. He dove onto the sled for a second run, and the runners collapsed under him in a dead stop. Goose slid off onto his belly and rolled down the remainder of the hill. The boys around him doubled over with uncontrollable laughter. After his humiliating tumble, Goose stood up and could not help but laugh, too.

During the walk home they all joked around and laughed about their adventures on Murphy's Hill. On the other hand, Dominick felt guilty as he deposited the remains of the borrowed sled onto the porch from where it was taken.

As the days followed, Dominick was so disturbed about what had happened to the sled that he began to save money from his paper route to purchase a new one. One late afternoon a few weeks later, without telling his friends, he went to the house and quietly placed an envelope containing the money through the mail slot of the front door then raced from the scene. He could now breathe easier and respect himself once again.

Reform School

By the time boys reached the age of fourteen, it was not uncommon for them to be doing a man's work. This was such the case with Dominick's brother, Tony. As a young boy, he gravitated to handling and caring for horses and would always find an excuse to ride alongside a neighborhood teamster while he delivered heavy freight.

Tony was a strong, strapping youth with the strength of an adult. He was consistently around horse-drawn wagons, either securing the horses or leading them to and from the stable. The men who owned the business appreciated his help and could rely on him to do everything and correctly. Tony was rewarded with the same pay as the other men, which a good portion he generously gave to his parents. Many missed days of school resulted. He thought it was far more important to work and earn money than to attend school. It was the law that every child should remain in school until the age of sixteen; inevitably, a truant officer began investigating Tony's whereabouts and found him working at the stables regularly. Though Tony was threatened with further action, he refused to attend school and continued to work anyway. The school authorities unanimously decided he was a habitual truant and ordered that he be reprimanded to a reformatory. Despite his parent's angry objection, he was taken into custody.

He was sentenced to a year and then transported to the nearest correctional school in the Borough. Giuseppe and Carolina were beside themselves with grief. Jimmy and Frank tried to relieve some of their parents' fears by informing them that Tony could defend and handle himself quite well, reminding them that in the past he had been victorious in fights, even when up against opponents three years his senior. The family had little choice but to accept and adjust to Tony's absence albeit with great difficulty.

The reformatory consisted of truants and delinquents of all sorts. Newly arrived Tony was escorted to the headmaster's office where he was informed that his time there would be tolerable or terrible, depending on his attitude. He agreed to obey the rules, for he realized punishment could be severe if he didn't.

With that brief introduction, he was led away and brought to the dormitory. Bunks were lined up on both sides as if in army barracks. After he was shown his sleeping bunk, the guards left, and within minutes, half a dozen boys approached him. Tony anticipated trouble. Three of them stepped closer and indicated that they were there to educate him. The boy closest to Tony swung at him, and Tony ducked to avoid it before hitting him with an upper cut to the jaw. The injured troublemaker flew head over heels backward over the bunk. The other two boys circled Tony as one of them took a swing at his face which Tony blocked with his forearm. He then attacked his assailant with a punch to the stomach instantly sending him to the floor. The remaining antagonist put his hands up and said he didn't want any trouble and backed away. Tony walked to the center of the room and stated, "Listen, I'm not looking for any trouble. I'm not a tough guy. All I want is to do my time, nothing else." A little puzzled, the other boys gave him a wide berth so he could return to his bunk.

By the next day, word had gotten out that the new guy made fast work of the three toughest kids in the dormitory. A few days later, while Tony was outside exercising with the others, it was obvious that everyone knew what had taken place, for there was an air of caution and respect for him. The first week went by without incident, which was fine for Tony.

One day a guard told him that Mr. Jacobs, the headmaster, wanted to see him and then escorted him to the office. Mr. Jacobs removed his spectacles, placed them on his desk, and then leaned back in his chair. "You've only been here a short time, and you have made a reputation for yourself. I am impressed. You don't come across as a troublemaker, but you won't run from a fight. I like that. Perhaps, we can help each other," the headmaster proposed.

"What do you have in mind?" Tony asked.

"Well, since the other boys already respect you, what do you think if I made you head monitor in charge of keeping the peace? You make sure everyone follows regulations to the letter. I know you cannot do this alone, so in a couple of days, I want you to select three other boys you can trust. What do you say?"

"Of course. It sounds good, but what am I going to get out of this?"

"I'm glad you asked that question. I like the fact you are right up front. If things work out, you will have added privileges such as returning home for a weekend every month. Also, more free time to do what you want during the day and unlimited access to the library. Best of all, I will take months off your stay here if things go well," Mr. Jacobs informed Tony.

"How could I refuse?" Tony asked with enthusiasm, adding, "Thank you. I will take the offer."

"By the way, the boys you choose will also be entitled to special privileges."

The following day, Tony decided upon who he could trust for the job. By that evening, the boys were aboard with the headmaster's proposal. Mr. Jacobs was delighted when he heard he had enlisted the others. This would directly result in less work and surveillance for the already overburdened guards, for the number of boys in the reformatory had reached capacity.

Months passed with relative calm, highlighted by letters from Tony's siblings which kept him abreast of family affairs. In his letters to them, Tony happily informed his loved ones that he would soon be allowed home one weekend a month. His parents wept with anticipation when they heard the good news.

With the help of Tony and his three allies, things ran smoothly to the relief of the school's authorities. There was a small group of malcontents who always tried to cause problems just to prove their presence. The most disruptive of which, was Butch, the very same delinquent who attacked Tony on his arrival. He had never forgotten Tony knocking him over his bunk and resentfully would try to instigate unrest between the boys of the school and the authorities. Butch rubbed most of the boys the wrong way and they were getting fed up with his underhanded methods; things heated up so much that they plotted to somehow get him. Butch realized his precarious situation and devised a plan to escape when the produce truck made its daily delivery.

He waited in the shadows until the truck slowly pulled away through the gate and then ran and jumped aboard, clinging to the door handles. Unknowingly, the driver continued on with the undetected additional cargo. Precisely at that moment, a group of boys passing by saw Butch make his escape and immediately notified Mr. Jacobs who then called upon Tony for help.

Mr. Jacobs, Tony, and a guard got into a car and chased after the runaway. Mr. Jacobs knew the truck's next delivery stop and anticipated the route to take. They sped to an intersection and saw the truck slow down to make a turn. At this point, Butch jumped off and broke into a run. When he thought he was safe enough, he slowed to a walk and mingled with the passersby. In close pursuit, Mr. Jacobs pulled to the curb. Tony then opened the car door and instantly took off.

Lost in the crowd, Butch was oblivious that he had been followed, and Tony slowed to a walk as to not alert him. Once in a while the culprit would nervously look over his shoulder. A trolley stopped at the corner to take on passengers, and Butch decided to get on line to get aboard. Tony nonchalantly walked to the line and stood a few feet behind him. Butch was about to step aboard when Tony reached past the person in front of him and grabbed Butch by the collar. He wrestled the quite surprised delinquent to the ground and held him there until Mr. Jacobs and the guard arrived and took Butch into custody.

Everyone at the reformatory heard about Butch's escape and Tony's effort in his capture. Most of the boys felt Butch had it coming for all of his past dirty deeds. As for Tony, Mr. Jacobs made good on his promise and gave him an extra weekend with his family.

Consequently, Tony's time was cut short by months for his good behavior and integrity. Before long, he returned home to his grateful family. He knew he would have to attend school until he was of legal age and then drop out. In time, he fulfilled his obligation and eventually returned to the stables and performed an honest man's work.

Shooting Dice

Of Dominick's brothers, Frank was the most industrious, shrewd, and street-smart. At a young age he was already gambling with cards and dice. He played so well that his competitors were usually older and more seasoned. On Sunday mornings a big dice game was always held on the sidewalk at the corner. Though Frank was still in his teens, he was a calculating and fearless player.

The group of players were recruited from all levels of the economic chain—day laborers, tradesmen, store owners, and professional gamblers. Knowing how to play and how to bet was vital. A good knowledge of the odds, and of course, having Lady Luck on your side was essential.

This time, Frank entered the game with forty dollars. Because the betting was high, this amount of money wouldn't last long if he should play badly. He bet with and against the one holding the dice, and in a short time, had increased his holdings to over two-hundred dollars. Luck was on his side, but his shrewd betting also contributed. Five, ten, and twenty dollar bills were jammed into his pockets as he continued to control the dice. The men around him were a little surprised at how this young guy could be such a seasoned player.

Within a half hour, Frank was holding more than a thousand dollars. Mickey Tomaro, one professional player in particular, was obviously upset with Frank's luck. Mickey suggested they go to another pair of dice. Frank nodded and said, "Sure, no problem," as a new pair of dice were opened and tossed to him.

Frank hit seven on the first throw and maintained his winning streak. The others shook their heads in disbelief. At this time, Dominick happened to walk by and see his brother in the center of the game with money bulging out of his pockets. Dominick was fearful for his brother's safety when he heard the chatter of disgruntled players. By now Frank's winnings had exceeded fifteen hundred dollars. His brother realized the potential danger and ran home to get help.

Dominick breathlessly burst into the house and informed his father and brothers Jimmy and Tony of Frank's predicament. The four of them were soon out the door.

The angels were with Frank that day, for Officer Patty Clancey came strolling toward the dice game twirling his police club. It was not his usual Sunday route but one he had chosen that day. He immediately spotted the game and advanced toward them shouting, "You're playin' dice on a Sunday, the Lord's day! You ought to be ashamed of yourselves, you good-for-nothing little bastards!" He raised his club as he rushed toward the gamblers to whack the nearest culprit.

"Cop's grab!" someone yelled, referring to the unwritten law among gamblers which gave them license to grab as much money as possible and run when a game was broken up by police. And this was precisely what everyone proceeded to do. For Frank, this was a stroke of phenomenal luck because the more seasoned players would have never allowed him to leave without giving them another chance to win back some of their money.

Frank ran toward home with his hands full of money and met his fathers and brothers halfway up the block. "Pop, there's no time for talk. Let's all get home first," Frank said before anyone else could speak. They all took his lead and hurried home.

When they arrived, Carolina and Rose were putting the finishing touches to Sunday dinner. "Pop," Frank addressed his father, "I've got a lot of money here."

"You do, and you're just a vagabond," scolded Giuseppe. "You gamble on God's day. I don't know who you take after. I do not want to talk to you now." Giuseppe turned and walked into the parlor, leaving the rest of the family in the kitchen.

Frank approached his mother and sister Rose and asked, "Will you two help count how much I won?" He proceeded to turn his pockets inside out and put the money in a pile which covered almost half of the kitchen table. Everyone in the family was stunned at the sight of ten and twenty dollar bills. At first, all just stood there and stared. No one had ever seen this amount of money at one time. After their amazement subsided, they began counting. With six people adding up the money, it only took a few minutes. The total sum was an astounding fourteen hundred and thirty dollars. There was enough money to pay for the rent for the next couple of years or buy a new car and still have some money left over. It was an unexpected windfall for the struggling immigrant family. Carolina remarked, "Your father is sometimes too good a man and loses his sense of reality. With this money, we can rest our minds and our hearts." The family agreed.

After he gave his mother a thousand dollars for the family's needs, Frank went on a spending spree with his share. He sported an assortment of new clothes, including suits, shirts, and shoes. He looked prosperous, and everyone noticed. Two days following the dice game, while Frank was with one of his friends, someone intentionally bumped into him. It turned out to be Mickey Tomaro, the heavy gambler who lost big. "Oh, I'm sorry, Frank," Tomaro quipped, "I thought I could shake loose some of the money I lost since you didn't give me a chance to win any back."

"Are you a wise guy?" Frank questioned, "Do you forget Patsy Kiernan broke up the game? You know better. It's the law of the streets. When the cops bust a game, it's over. Period."

"I don't think it's over," Mickey corrected him. "I demand another game, just you and me."

"I don't like your attitude. I don't have to do anything just because you're a sore loser. Move along, Mickey. Don't make an ass out of yourself. Keep moving, and I'll forget you banged into me intentionally to instigate something."

"You know, Frank, you're right. I think we should settle this now."

"Okay, Mickey. Right here. Right now. Let's go," Frank challenged him. They both shed their jackets and caps and rolled up their shirt sleeves as they squared off to fight. Mickey was a strong, stocky brute while Frank was thirty pounds lighter and a good boxer.

Mickey charged head first and swung a heavy right to Frank's head, but it was deflected by Frank's forearms protecting his face. This was quickly followed by another swing which hit Frank's kidney when he turned to avoid the blow. Mickey knew he had hurt him and got in closer for another shot. This time, Frank was able to duck out of the way, and Mickey almost lost his balance as he missed. Frank took advantage of the situation and managed to hit him in the jaw. Obviously stunned, Mickey shook his head and stumbled backward but remained on his feet. Frank let him recover and danced around him as blood dripped from his mouth. Mickey wiped the blood with the back of his hand and charged Frank like a bull. Frank sidestepped to avoid him. As Mickey went by him, Frank swung and hit him on the side of the head. Mickey's ear took the full force of the blow, blood spurting.

Down the block, Bach and Red walked up to investigate

the commotion. When they realized it was Frank involved in the fight, they ran to get Dominick. When they arrived at the house, they told Dominick what was taking place down the street. Dominick and Tony immediately ran to the scene with Bach and Red. They pushed their way through the small crowd that had gathered. When in full view, they saw Mickey with a blood-stained shirt trying to go after an unmarked Frank once more. Frank was still energetic, and Mickey, though stronger and bigger, was outmatched. This was a dilemma for Dominick, for he had been friends with Mickey in the past and didn't want to see him get hurt any further. But Mickey was too bullheaded to give up. Dominick whispered into Tony's ear, "We have to do something," and then asked Mickey to stop. Tony went to Frank and grabbed him in a bear hold.

"Stop it, Frank," Tony said. "He's done. No more." Fortunately, Dominick was able to convince Mickey to finally call it quits.

From that time on, the two adversaries came to an understanding to keep their distance from each other. The unspoken truce would remain in place for years as Frank and Mickey went on with their lives.

Prospect Park and the Raft

On a sultry summer morning, the boys discussed what to do that day. All suggestions up until then were knocked down because they had already been done repeatedly. Joey finally came up with a novel idea to make a raft and float it in the lake at Prospect Park. They all laughed at first until Red said, "Maybe it isn't as nuts as it sounds. I bet we can find enough junk wood to make somethin'."

"It beats hanging around here and doing the same old stuff," Dominick added. The rest of the gang agreed. Bach was the first to go home and get a hatchet and rope. The others did the same and returned with hammers, nails, and plenty of ambition. After they met up with each other, they started their mile and a half walk to the park. On the way they planned on how to construct their makeshift raft.

During their walk, they remained on the lookout for anything they could scavenge. Bach and Joey spied a long board behind garbage cans and reacted as if they had found the Golden Fleece. The happy, optimistic adventurers continued on their way along Troy Ave. and made a right onto Empire Blvd. and then continued the straight run to Prospect Park. Passersby glanced whimsically in their direction as the boys gathered odd looking pieces of debris along the busy thoroughfare.

They finally arrived at the park's entrance at the intersection of Empire and Flatbush. They tried to look inconspicuous as they made a sharp left toward the lake. The boys split up into twos at the shoreline as they gathered anything else which would further help them.

Less than a half hour later, the boys reassembled to access their materials and soon realized their best method of constructing their raft was to lash the logs and planks together with rope. They weaved it over and under their wooden pieces. It took under an hour for them to try it out in shallow water.

Dominick and Joey boarded the craft as the rest of the boys gave it a good push out into the water. Dominick, using a long pole, was able to steer it in the desired direction. This worked well as long as the pole could touch the bottom; it also limited the raft to the shallows. For taking it into deeper water, they would have to devise another way to control it.

After navigating the edge of the lake successfully, Dominick and Joey returned to the shore to pick up the rest of their friends. Once aboard, they poled their way to a not-so-busy area of the lake. Everything seemed to be going well and the raft held together; it even outperformed their expectations. The boys were beside themselves with joy as they ventured into deeper water and imagined themselves as pirates on the high seas. They were too busy having fun to notice the raft heading to the middle of the lake. This was not a problem until the poles could no longer touch the bottom and they lost control of the direction. They began to drift to wherever the current flowed. Unable to steer, they approached an area of the lake which was frequented by a number of rented rowboats. Boaters soon scurried out of their way and screamed obscenities. Young couples out for a romantic afternoon were now dodging the out of control raft manned by half a dozen unruly kids. The boys headed wherever the wind and current flowed strongest.

During much of the time they had many close encounters with unfortunate rowboats that happened to glide too close. Side-swiping and unintentional ramming by the raft created chaos on the lake. Two young men saw the scared boys' predicament and rowed over to help. One of them yelled out, "Boys, you will have to be towed. It's the only way out of this! Do you have a rope aboard?"

"We have about twenty feet of clothesline!" Red shouted back.

"That will do it," one of the men answered, "Just secure it to the raft." Dominick and Red moved quickly and looped a line around the main log, and after tying a knot, they were ready to be towed. Each of the men in the rowboat manned an oar and rowed with as much strength as possible. The boys cheered as they glided behind the rescue team. Soon the kids and the ill-fated craft reached the safety of the shore.

When the raft halted, the happy youths splashed through the water up to their knees and patted their rescuers on the back with gratitude for their help. The men told the boys to pull the raft ashore as far as they could. The boys nodded and then dragged it into the bushes.

The would-be-adventurers said goodbye to the helpful men and quickly moved away from the lake before park officials could respond to the disturbance. On their way home they all agreed to think things out before they jumped into another grand scheme.

Summer Exploits

Every few years horses were brought directly into Manhattan from the west on railroad cattle cars accompanied by cowboys. They were to replace the aging horses of the mounted police in the precincts throughout the five boroughs. From the railroad yards the horses were driven by wranglers then through the city streets to their destinations. The day before they would pass through the streets of Brooklyn, the local police would notify the businesses and the people along the proposed route. An hour before the horses' approximate arrival, all vehicles and wagons were to be temporarily removed from that area in order to free up the roads. The store owners cleared away any curbside barrels and crates. Adults and children alike looked forward to seeing the unique and exciting spectacle. All of the neighborhood kids vied for the best seats on the stoops in front of the houses overlooking the street. The adults smiled at the children's enthusiasm, for some had positioned themselves hours before the event. The atmosphere was festive, for most people knew times were quickly changing, and it was inevitable that the whole event would someday vanish. To pass away the time, Dominick and his friends played cards and other games, looking over their shoulders every so often toward the end of the block to catch any indication of the horses' arrival. The boys finally overheard one of the local men tell another that the mustangs had been cited three streets away. The kids cheered when they heard the good news and stood in the center of the street. They squinted to see any advancing images. Goose and Red heard what they thought was a shot. Everyone was on edge when they heard the sound of a second shot, sharp and distinctive. "That's them!" Dominick shouted to his friends with happiness, "Do you remember the last time? It's the crack of their whips that sound like gun shots!"

"You're right," Bach said, "I can make out the cowboys and the mustangs now! Look!" Again the cracks of the whips sounded as the cowboys came into view. Anticipating their momentary arrival, the excited kids moved out of the street beyond the curb and back to the front steps for safety. The clamor of the horses' hooves hitting the cobblestone street grew louder, and the increasing thunder of the herd almost resembled a small earthquake. Empty barrels and containers near the houses began to rattle and vibrate. In moments, the mustangs and the whip-cracking cowboys were directly in full view, and everyone was in awe. The sight of drovers sitting on their oiled saddles with their leather boots, shining stirrups, and colorful shirts excited the boys so much they could barely contain themselves. All the western movies they had seen on the screen paled in comparison to the reality in front of them. The herd of horses seemingly passed the crowd with a blink of an eye, and too soon everyone watched the last mustang gallop by. The boys returned to the center of the street to get one last look as the horses disappeared from view. As other years before, people of the neighborhood were completely fascinated by what they had just witnessed and a little saddened, too, by its brevity.

On a lighter note, not to waste anything, some old timers rushed out with shovels in hand to gather the manure left behind in the streets and scooped it up for their backyard gardens.

The boys were so greatly impressed that they could not stop talking about it for days. When they got together, some of them talked about going out west someday. While most were content to dream about it, Bach planned on completing school and going cross country even if he had to skip the rail to do so.

On a cool morning, the boys assembled on the corner at 9 a.m. to go to Farante's Farm. Each brought something essential to have a good time. Bach brought his father's fishing line and hooks; Red was able to grab five good sized potatoes from his mother's pantry. Dominick's mother Carolina had just baked bread and allowed him to take two loaves. Joey contributed half a dozen onions and

113

the same amount of ripe tomatoes. Not to be outdone, Goose added two small salamis to the cache. He also borrowed a small frying pan to fry any fish they might be able to catch.

They stuffed all of the items into burlap sacks which they slung over their shoulders as they got underway to the farm. The optimistic boys easily traversed block after city block as they continued on their trek. When they reached the outer edge of Farante's, they walked to the northwest section where a fast-flowing stream separated the land from a thick wooded area. There the boys would make their camp for the day. They climbed over the wood rail fence, oblivious to the farm animals nearby.

Bach and Red couldn't wait to put their fishing lines in the water in hope of catching a sunny or two. Meanwhile, Dominick, Joey, and Goose searched for dry, fallen branches and gathered rocks for a fire circle. In a short time they had a roaring blaze.

With frying pan in hand, Goose was more than ready to fry some fresh fish. This did not seem likely, for Red and Bach kept losing their catch when they tried to remove the fish from the hooks. The slippery little devils wiggled right back into the water. Finally, after numerous attempts, Bach was successful in hooking one and holding onto it. Red, on the other hand, was not as lucky. After almost an hour without success, he put his fishing line aside and gave up. In frustration, he picked up rocks and began tossing them at the elusive fish. He quickly realized this tactic would not be fruitful either. He threw his arms up in disgust and walked through ankle-deep water toward camp when he almost fell over when he stepped on something. He bent over for a closer look and widened his eyes with disbelief. A fish was floundering right under his foot. After realizing that he had somehow stepped on it, he proceeded to render it lifeless. He held up his trophy, and his friends laughed at his phenomenal luck. They now had two fish to fry.

Goose immediately cleaned and gutted the sunnies with his pen knife. Though small, they were good additions to the food the boys had already brought and would prove enough to satisfy their appetites.

The boys sat around the fire after they had eaten and talked over what to do next. They liked the idea of a campfire, but the sun was extra hot that day, and they decided to take off their shoes and socks to cool off in the stream. They shrieked and flayed their arms when the frigid water touched their skin. Dominick unintentionally splashed Joey, and before they knew it, a spirited water fight ensued. Regardless of the instigator of it all, they splashed each other with abandon. Soon they were soaked to the bone and laughing without a care. The boys knew they had to dry off before going home as they were certain it would not go well with their mothers.

They chose a verdant hillside facing the afternoon sun, and each selected a comfortable spot to stretch out spread eagle to dry their clothes. In twenty minutes, all the boys were sound asleep and unaware of their surroundings. An hour passed before a noisy group of ravens disturbed Dominick. He looked up and saw the birds perched in a nearby tree and then drifted back to sleep. He was again awakened a little while later by the same boisterous birds, but this time their chatter was more frantic than before. The others awoke and rubbed their eyes, puzzled by the ravens' raucous behavior.

Dominick was the first to rise to his feet and look around. To his astonishment, he set his eyes on a large, menacing bull standing not more than a hundred yards away. The animal was pawing the ground with his foreleg and getting ready to charge. "Let's go!" Dominick shouted urgently. "Run!"

The boys sprang up and sprinted toward the fence a few hundred feet away. The bull didn't hesitate to break into a full run in their direction.

"Oh, crap!" Goose yelled, running so fast that he almost tripped over his own feet.

"Legs, don't fail me now!" Bach mumbled to himself as he made his way through the grass. Despite the boys' head start, the irate bull quickly made up the distance between them.

"When we get to the fence, just jump over!" Red shouted as he and the rest of the gang were about seventy-five feet from the fence. He and Dominick were the first to get there and pushed off the bottom rail simultaneously before diving over. Goose followed right behind and then over as Red and Dominick helped pull him to safety. They all did the same for smaller Joey and Bach. Not a second too soon, the bull charged to the fence and then halted. Safe and sighing relief, the boys brushed themselves off and got a good look at the still-snorting bull standing a few feet away.

They talked on the way home about their harrowing escape and how fortunate they were that no one was hurt. They were still shaking their heads in disbelief when they arrived back in the neighborhood.

Dominick returned just as supper was being placed on table. Jimmy, already seated, looked up at his little brother and asked, "Hey, Dom, your clothes look wrinkled. Did you get caught in a thunderstorm?"

"Yeah, I did get wct,"" Dominick answered breathlessly.

"Anything interesting happen today?" Jimmy asked with a knowing smile.

"Not really. Same old stuff." Dominick turned and smiled to himself.

The Long Haul

The heavy freight trucks of the time were a challenge at first for Tony, but he soon adapted. He routinely traveled to Philadelphia, Hartford, and Providence, and the routine usually involved being away a night or two. He would often pull on the side of a road and sleep in the truck. The primitive roadways were devoid of street lights which made traveling at night precarious. The vehicles were equipped with headlamps, but the lights were dim and did not throw much illumination on the dark, country lanes. Operating these trucks for long hours was tedious and required a high level of concentration. The constant worry about the freight shifting took its toll on the lone drivers.

During the year, Tony would periodically ask one of his brothers to accompany him on some of the long trips. Frank would go if he was not working, and Dominick would take his place if he didn't have school. Dominick loved the country and saw the long trips with Tony as adventurous interludes and a welcome escape from the hectic, crowded city. Their mother provided an ample supply of food which made it a better time. She made their favorite fried eggplant sandwiches on homemade crusty bread and wrapped them in wax paper. The food was placed in a metal wash tub filled with ice to prevent spoilage.

One early fall morning, teenaged Dominick and his brother Tony rose early at 5 a.m. and ate a quick breakfast. Tony then left and walked two blocks to get the truck. He returned twenty minutes later to pick up his brother and the food. They would be transporting large bundles of cotton rags used by manufacturers in their cleanup of machine oils, and the heavy bales were secured tightly to the flatbed of the truck. After saying goodbye and securing their provisions, the two young men pulled away.

Not long into the drive, they stopped at an intersection, and Tony glanced at his excited brother. He reached over and playfully touseled Dominick's hair. A glint of amusement flickered in Tony's eyes as he smiled at Dominick's enthusiasm. They made a left onto Atlantic Ave. and noticed the absence of cars and trucks on the usually busy street. It was still early. They passed the occasional horse-drawn wagon on its way to an open-air market. These early bird travelers picked up and delivered produce from local farms. Soon the two brothers reached Flatbush Ave. where the majority of the traffic headed toward the East River and the Manhattan Bridge. The din of honking cars and chain-driven trucks pervaded the air. The commotion of the city evolved into a loud crescendo as they approached the bridge. Dominick marveled at its massive construction and observed the river below. The morning sun reflected off the dark, silky water as they crossed the bridge and merged into the busy streets of Manhattan. The clanging of trolley cars and the noise of the city was an instant, abrasive annoyance. Tony shook his head and said, "Dom, we'll be leaving all this in a short while."

"And I thought Brooklyn was bad," Dominick answered.

The avenues were crowded with Italian and Jewish vendors selling food from push carts. Other merchants had kitchen wares for sale along with an array of clothing items. They threaded their way with caution through the hectic masses without mishap.

They left the city limits and traveled north toward quieter Harlem and the Bronx. Open spaces and trees became more common as they crossed the Harlem River. They continued north to the King's Bridge section to pick up Old Boston Post Rd. They would periodically stop to inspect the cargo and make sure nothing was loosened during the drive.

The scenery began to slowly transform from urban to country, none too soon for Dominick who preferred a more pastoral setting. They drove eastward on Boston Rd. toward Long Island Sound, passing through New Rochelle and Larchmont on the way to the city of Rye. A clear view of the sound was visible along the route, its beauty dotted with small fishing crafts and pleasure boats. This scene became frequent as the road hugged the coast. They made good time traveling through Mamareck heading northeast.

They drove through Rye and approached Greenwich, Connecticut where they stopped at a filling station and purchased gasoline. Soon they were back on the road with what seemed an endless panoramic view of the sound. The miles slid by easily. They passed through the quaint cities of Bridgeport, New Haven, and New London almost unnoticed while the two brothers chatted about their lives and caught up with each other's everyday happenings. They entered Old Mystic Seaport and figured it would be an excellent place to stop, check the cargo, and eat lunch.

They parked on top of a hill overlooking the old seaport and anxiously tore into their food stash graciously prepared by their mother. From this vantage point they spied a few sailing ships still docked at the port. Dominick was impressed with the old ships that were once used as whalers. He had read in many novels about men who had ventured out to sea in such vessels, and he secretly longed to investigate the old ships and have adventures on the waves.

An hour had already gone by before the young men prepared for the rest of their journey. They departed with a little hesitation as Dominick took one last look. He promised himself he would someday return and spend more time taking in the historic sights and the significance of their history.

They left Mystic behind and went on their way toward Providence, Rhode Island. They never lost sight of the ocean, and if so, only for a very brief period of time. The smallest state of the Union offered pristine vistas of both countryside and sea, and they were soon driving through the outer limits of Providence.

It was a busy hub of activity, and it seemed as if all roads merged here. After some clever maneuvering, Tony emerged on the far side of the city where they picked up the old road once again and continued to Boston. They passed rolling hills dotted with small farms on their route northward.

Once in Boston, they traveled along a road that paralleled the Charles River. To Dominick's delight, they passed Fenway Park, the home of the famed Boston Red Sox. After a few blocks, Tony turned into an area of many manufacturing companies and backed up the truck to a loading platform. The foreman checked Tony's invoice and then informed him that it was fine to leave the goods there. Soon other workers started to unload the heavy bales of cloth.

After the freight was unloaded, the two brothers hopped back up into the truck and began their return trip. Despite Dominick's protests about leaving Boston so soon, Tony decided to get back on the road before dark. Defeated, Dominick leaned his head and closed his eyes knowing the long trip ahead. It wasn't long until the boy dozed off.

Hours later, Tony pulled to the side of the road for that evening's respite and nudged Dominick. "It's a safe place to spend the night." Dominick woke and shrugged without enthusiasm. "Look, Dom, I'm really sorry about cutting the time short. I know you wanted to see more of Boston. Maybe next time. Come on, let's eat something."

They watched the moon rise and ate in silence. The surrounding landscape quickly became imbued with a silver glow, revealing tall wildflowers in a nearby meadow. "So, Dom, what do you see yourself doing in the future? I know you love to read. Maybe an office career? I know Jimmy and Pop think you have what it takes to go into law."

"Gee, I don't know. Maybe a writer."

"That sure beats hauling freight. Do what you can to make something better for yourself."

"Think you'll marry that girl?"

"Molly?" Dominick nodded.

"Maybe. How 'bout you? Any girls catch your eye?" Tony mussed his brother's hair and hugged him around the neck. Dominick dropped his head with a smile.

"Maybe." Dominick laughed.

"Speaking of marriage, I guess our sister Rose will probably marry Joe. He's been taking her out a lot, and he's a good guy."

"Momma's gonna miss her."

"Yeah, she puts up with all of us boys. I wish I could make it easier for her sometimes."

"Me, too," Dominick agreed. A few moments of quiet ensued as they both listened to the night sounds—insects in the fields and the occasional night bird.

They decided to call it a day. After locking the doors of the truck, they reached behind their seats and grabbed two blankets to ward off any night chill. Though it was not yet fall, the temperature in the hills could drop. It wasn't long until both brothers were sound asleep as late summer harmonies drifted in through the lowered windows.

During the night, an eerie shriek startled Dominick, and he nudged Tony. The screech came again. Tony smiled. "It's okay. It's only a screech owl. They sound like screaming women, but they're harmless. Go back to sleep." Tony's words were reassuring, but the country sounds were a little unnerving for a city boy.

An hour later, Dominick was again awakened, this time by the yelps of a young coyote. He realized they were safe inside the truck and dismissed his fears. He tried to go back to sleep by remembering the sailing ships of Mystic, Connecticut.

A little after sunrise, both Dominick and Tony were jolted by the loud cry of a raven that had perched on the hood of the truck. The bird continued his abrasive scolding and was apparently upset by the presence of the two unwelcome human intruders. After a while, the brothers gave up on going back to sleep. They rubbed their eyes and stretched the sleep from their limbs and decided to get back on the road.

They retraced their route and came upon their points of interest as they traveled through Connecticut. Tony, ahead of schedule, allowed an hour for Dominick's curiosity to be quelled by watching the seaport.

Too soon, they were on their way again, and mile after mile drifted by unnoticed. They were back in New York state once again and from there it would only be an hour or so to home.

After crossing the Manhattan Bridge, they made their way toward the old neighborhood. Tony turned right onto Troy where one of his friends was busy unloading blocks of ice. It was Big Mike, strong as an ox with a gentle spirit. Tony beeped the horn, and Mike turned around with a broad smile and waved back. As Tony made a left onto St. Mark's, Dominick saw his friends hanging out at the corner. Tony beeped again as they passed the boys. Bach, Red, and Danny popped their heads up from playing cards and waved when they realized Dominick was in the truck. "Hey, come on down if you got time!" Red yelled out.

"See you guys later!" Dominick yelled back with a big smile.

Tony pulled up in front of their house, and Carolina parted the curtains. She was happy to see both her sons safely home again.

Ghost Stories

Halloween was fast approaching, and Dominick's school was already festive with the hallways and classrooms displaying student's drawings of pumpkins, green-faced witches, and cut-out paper ghosts. There was an air of intrigue and haunting anticipation as teachers read Washington Irving's *Legend of Sleepy Hollow* to the children's delight. It stirred their imaginations with mystery and wonder, especially Dominick.

It was not surprising that the neighborhood boys were preoccupied with all things Halloween. Some pestered their parents for days about getting pumpkins to carve which resulted in a majority of parents finally giving in just to stop the whining. As in other years past, an unofficial contest ensued between neighbors and it wasn't long until Dominick's street was abuzz with who could produce the largest or most artistic jack-o-lantern. Competition became contagious as the older brothers and sisters volunteered their help and ideas.

When the kids of St. Mark's Ave. found time to congregate during the week of Halloween, they exchanged ghost stories. Bach in particular was very good at telling a frightening tale. In their group, Goose—not very bright and the most impressionable—was easily intimidated by the stories, and his friends knew it. One night Dominick, Red, and Bach planned a Halloween prank and climbed a high fence behind Goose's house. Red dressed as the quintessential ghost with a white sheet and holes for eyes and positioned himself in the shadows on top of the fence. Dominick and Bach remained below to lend moral support. In a low, breathy voice, Red called out, "Goooose, where are you?" Dominick and Bach held in their laughter as Goose lifted his bedroom window. "Goooose, where are you?" the voice came again. This time Goose caught a glimpse of the white spirit hovering over the fence.

"Pop!" Goose yelled for his father, but by the time his father responded, Red had climbed down out of sight. The three boys did all they could to not break up laughing.

"Son, you must be seeing things," Goose's father concluded after looking out the window and seeing nothing.

"But Pop, I know what I saw!" Goose persisted.

The following day, when the boys were together, Goose told everyone what had happened to him the night before. The three culprits feigned surprised and tried to refrain from bursting into laughter. His friends admitted to believing in ghosts and that it could happen.

That night, the mischievous trio returned to Goose's house. As he had done the night before, Red put on the sheet and took his place on the fence. "Goooose, I know you're there...come on out...," he moaned in his best ghostly voice. But this time when the window opened, it wasn't Goose but his father. Before Red could move out of the way, Goose's father heaved a heavy leather work boot in his direction which hit him square in the chest, and he fell backward off the fence.

Fortunately, Dominick and Bach broke his fall, and he wasn't hurt from the tumble, but his chest would have a good bruise. They ran from the scene, retreating into the shadows of the night.

A few nights after Halloween, buttoned up in jackets, Dominick and the gang played cards under the street light with their breath puffing into the cool air. Something caught Bach's attention in the middle of the block, and he squinted to get a better view. He scanned the street but saw nothing. His eyes returned to the cards. Joey, sitting opposite of him, glanced up and remarked, "What the heck is Rocco's produce wagon doing here at this time?"

"What are you seeing things? I don't see anything," Red answered, looking around.

"Wait," Dominick said, "I see it. Over there..." He pointed.

"What are you trying to do, scare me? I'm not a dope. I

don't see nothin', cut it out," Goose said. Dominick and Joey continued to observe Rocco while the two other boys were beginning to be annoyed at their distracted friends. Shortly after, when it was getting late, they broke up the game and headed toward home.

Dominick walked alongside Joey and frequently turned around to look over his shoulder. "Boy, that was weird," he said. "How could they not see Rocco?"

"I don't know. I'll see you tomorrow," Joey said when they reached his house.

"See ya." Dominick turned and walked toward home in the direction of Rocco's wagon. When he got to his front steps, he stopped and took a closer look. He saw Rocco looking at him from the wagon. The old peddler then raised his arm, acknowledging the boy. Dominick waved in return and then disappeared into his house. Once inside, Dominick presumed Rocco had some business or was visiting a friend at that hour.

Dominick went into the kitchen and found his sister Rose at the table drinking a cup of tea. He told her the story and how he and Joey were the only ones to see old Rocco. Rose reassured him. "Dominick, it was a dark night. Maybe the others were so intent on playing cards that just didn't see him. Don't worry about it. Have a good night's sleep." She kissed him goodnight.

"You're probably right." Dominick shrugged his shoulders. "It was pretty dark, and they might have missed seeing him if they didn't look in the right direction. Thanks Rose. See ya in the morning."

The following day, Dominick, Red, Bach, and Joey sat on the wide steps outside the tobacco store and waited for the rest of their friends. Since it was Saturday, the boys talked over what they might do that afternoon and watched men go in and out of the store with newspapers and cigars in hand. The boys dropped their plans when an outside conversation between two people caught their attention. "Gee, it's too bad what happened yesterday. Poor Rocco the peddler," one man remarked.

"What do you mean?" the other asked.

"A large truck ran into his wagon, and he was killed. His horse had to be put down." Stunned, Dominick looked at Joey.

"Did you hear that?" Dominick asked. Joey nodded nervously and then they both went into the store to buy a few copies of the paper so they could read about the accident.

Red and the others were astonished to read the news and remembering what Dominick and Joey had seen the previous evening. Dominick left his friends and ran home with the newspapers. He pushed the door open and waved the paper at Rose and their parents. They were all surprised and saddened to hear what had happened, especially his sister. "Dominick, don't be alarmed," Rose advised, adding, "Rocco must have shown himself to those who were receptive. In his way, he let us know that our spirits go on. It may have been his way of saying goodbye to the people he knew in this life."

One day in November, Red delivered groceries to a

gentleman who would hunt rabbit in rural Long Island, and in appreciation for Red's dependable service, gave the boy a rabbit he had shot a day earlier. Rabbit was not a meal easy to come by, and Red was excited to bring it home for his mother to cook, one of her favorites. He knew she would roast it in tomatoes and rosemary, just like the locals had done during her youth in southern Italy where they commonly called it cacciatore or hunter's style.

That evening his mother presented the delicious feast to her husband and two sons. They were disappointed that their landlady, Widow Grimaldi who lived downstairs, was unable to accept their invitation, for she had other plans that night. Nonetheless, everyone heartily indulged themselves.

After enjoying the meal, Red's mother cleared the table while the rest of the family remained seated and talked about their day. Red's father set down a half-filled glass of wine, and extraordinarily, as he was talking, his glass mysteriously moved across the table and then back again. He immediately pushed his chair back and looked at his sons. "What did you do? Are you playing games? I don't like it," he remarked.

"Pop, I didn't do anything. And neither did Eddie," Red said, his brother nodding in agreement. Their father slowly and cautiously picked up the glass to see if it was wet. He thought maybe if it had been wet that it might have slid across the smooth tabletop when he set it down. He soon realized it was not the case. He stood up in amazement, befuddled by what had just taken place. Red's mother who had not witnessed it spoke up.

"Hey, you probably put the glass down so forcefully that it just slid across the table," she said with annoyance.

"Cara mia, believe me, I did not. And the bottom of the glass was not wet. The table was dry."

"Maybe you had too much wine to drink," his wife scoffed.

"So the boys are drunk, too? They saw what just happened. And they certainly had no wine to drink."

Red met up with his friends the next day and told them what had happened the night before at the dinner table. Bach perked up and said, "Boy, a lot of unexplainable things have happened around here the past couple of weeks."

"Yeah, a lot of weird stuff," Dominick agreed.

"You guys are doin' it again," Goose interrupted them, "You're always tryin' to scare me. Stop it and let's talk about something else."

They all left the neighborhood and trekked a couple of miles to hang out at a nearby farm. They played cowboys and Indians for about an hour or two and then explored the woods bordering the pastures. They imagined themselves as early explorers, and after a few hours, decided to start heading home. They heard an ominous screeching coming from behind them as they emerged from the woods. Before anyone else could even react, Goose raced by his friends, hightailing it back home. Not knowing what had made the awful sound, the rest of the boys broke out into a full sprint after Goose. They didn't stop running until they saw their familiar safety of their neighborhood. They regrouped in front of Red's house and chatted about what they had heard in the woods. Not one of them could identify the eerie sound that had spooked them. "What happened, you guys?" asked Goose. "Are you afraid of somethin'? I thought I was the only scaredy cat. I guess not. You all got scared, too. That's a good one!" He chuckled. Not one of his friends said a word to refute his claim, and the boys broke up to go home and eat supper.

Red entered his house to find his parents speaking about the conversation his mother had with the landlady, the widow Grimaldi. Apparently, when his mother had commented about the crazy incident with the wine glass on the table, Mrs. Grimaldi laughed a little and said, "Oh, that's just my dead husband fooling around. His favorite meal was roasted rabbit, and he was probably showing you how much he liked it." When Red's father heard about Mrs. Grimaldi's response, he told his wife it would be the last time they would ever eat rabbit and to inquire what else Mr. Grimaldi liked so she would be sure to never prepare it.

Neighborhood Sustenance

Three Italian immigrant men shared a house together a few doors from Dominick's home. They lived as frugally as possible and sent as much money as they could afford to their struggling families back in Italy. Giovanni, one of the men from Calabria, was a tailor who made fine clothes and was employed by a company who sold custom suits in Manhattan. Gregorio, one of the others, was a shoemaker, and he, too, was from Reggio, the same Calabrian town as Giovanni and was the most recent arrival to America. He worked in the same building where Dominick's father was also employed. He was a good craftsman and well thought of in the workplace. The last of the trio was Stephano who arrived from Naples years before. He was a long shoreman who worked on the Brooklyn docks as a foreman of a small gang of workers, a tough but reliable individual.

134

One common bond among the three men was their flare for cooking. The daily preparation of meals, as well as the household chores was divided among them. There was a fourth personality who also resided there, a very vocal and precocious feathered cuss named Figaro. The green African parrot was acquired by Stephano from a seaman years before. The talkative bird accompanied him wherever he traveled, and the little creature was a popular resident of the neighborhood. Everyone who came in contact with him could not help but be amused by his many antics. In warmer weather, everyone could hear his chatter when the windows were open. He was tethered to a wooden perch that overlooked the street. Any person or animal that walked in front of the window became the target of Figaro's relentless criticism. His vocabulary, along with his variety of calls and whistles, was quite impressive.

The daily deliverymen and peddlers were especially vulnerable to his verbal assaults, and his cleverness was demonstrated most noisily when the ice or milkman left his wagon to put something on the doorstep. He would whistle, which was an immediate signal to the horse to move forward. Though comical, this did not go well for the deliverymen who had to chase after their wagons. Of course, the kids of the neighborhood adored Figaro and would call to him when they walked by his window to get his attention. The bird would react with colorful words or sharp whistles. If Figaro saw someone who did not fit his tastes, he would launch into profanity that would embarrass a sailor. He did not like two older women in particular, and it was an ongoing confrontation whenever they walked by on their way to the market. Curse words were hurled at them, and they would respond by yelling back and clenching their hands between their teeth to keep their tempers in check. It was hysterically funny to any onlooker. So intimidated by his wrath, some people would cross the street to avoid him altogether. Some complained to Stephano about the bird's tirades, and he would say, "Wella, he's a smarta, frisky sunnova gun. There's not mucha I canna do. Just stay away fromma him and don'ta get him mad." In frustration, the victims of Figaro's moods would then throw their hands up in exasperation and angrily walk away.

Time and time again, visitors unaware of Figaro would knock on the door. "Is there anyone home?" they would ask and repeat it after no response.

"Nobody'sa home!" Figaro would finally respond in his Old Country dialect. The visitors would then insist the door be opened. When the door was not opened, the dialogue would continue.

"If you're home, open the door!"

"Nobody'sa home!" Figaro would say again until the callers eventually left shaking their heads in disbelief and frustration.

Home alone for most of the day, Figaro was quite content with entertaining himself without an audience. Through the years, his presence and that of the three men added much life and color to the ever-changing neighborhood.

A few doors down from the Donato family, on the same

136

side of the street lived the Regerrios. They made good use of a vacant lot adjacent to their house by transforming it into a large, fertile garden. Mr. Regerrio, with the help of his family, grew the staples of any good Italian garden—meaty tomatoes, colorful peppers, large eggplants, and an array of herbs including basil and mint. Those who walked by were treated to the sweet, fresh aromas that wafted into the street. The garden with rows of manicured plants was lovingly maintained by Mrs. Regerrio and their children during the day, and in the evening, by Mr. Regerrio when he returned home from work. There he would retreat and water the thirsty plants after sundown.

By the end of June, squash and lettuces were ready to pick and not only made their way to the family table but to friends in the neighborhood. The later yield of eggplants, peppers, and finally, tomatoes, were canned and sometimes dried for future use. Another portion of the produce was used to barter for goods and services.

Everyone who took part in the family's annual bounty hated to see the inevitable waning of the growing season. Too soon clean-up was in full swing, and the Regerrios were clearing the garden, pulling out roots, and adding manure to prepare the soil for the following year.

Mr. Regerrio's next project for the family would be the yearly task of wine-making. His hand-operated wine press located in the cellar had been made with salvaged parts from the junkyard, and his ingenuity and relentless desire to preserve Old Country traditions was his passion. Each year, he ordered one hundred cases of grapes from upstate New York through an ad in the newspaper, and within two weeks, the greatly-anticipated shipment was delivered curbside. Mr. Regerrio, his two sons, and a few neighborhood kids including Dominick would help carry the crates of fruit to an open cellar window and slide them through a coal chute into the basement. The crates were stacked chest-high around the perimeter of the cellar and wherever space was available. The perfume of the autumnal bounty filled the dark, musty space with the promise of wine.

Saturday would be spent removing the grapes from their wooden boxes and flushing five oak barrels clean. Large bunches of burgundy grapes were piled into the upper part of the wine press, and everyone had an opportunity to turn the wheel. Instantly, the sound of the precious liquid began to flow into waiting buckets and then poured into the barrels to begin its journey to becoming wine.

Within a week, all of the grapes were pressed, and the barrels sealed. Months later, when the wine was ready to drink, friends were invited, and they all gathered around a long table in the cellar as the barrels were tapped. Tasting of the wine continued a treasured centuries-old tradition.

Another family that added color to the block was the large Grazziano clan consisting of six sons and five daughters. It was imperative that the parents devised alternative methods of providing enough food to go around. Their two story wood frame house and ample building behind solved their dilemma. In the outbuilding, Mr. Grazziano fitted shelves designed to accommodate roosts for dozens of chickens. To increase the production of eggs, he converted the basement to house twenty-five to thirty more hens. The eggs provided a healthy food source for the always hungry kids. One thing that was not appreciated by everyone was the early morning chorus of boisterous roosters informing the neighbors that it was the beginning of a new day. Most people did not mind, for many were originally from rural sections of Italy, but there were always a few who were constantly irritated, though the steady supply of fresh eggs made any inconvenience tolerable.

Another contributor to daily substance was Mr. Romano who operated a bakery a few blocks away on Utica Ave. and also had a brick oven in his home. He and his eldest son made hearty loaves of bread for family and friends. Various hard woods were burned and produced the fiery embers needed to make the thick-crusted breads which were sold but also given to struggling neighbors. The aroma of semolina and whole grain loaves tantalized neighbors and passersby alike. Many local homes were blessed to have the delicious staple on their tables.

During the cooler months of autumn and winter, people frequented the Romano basement and gathered around the warmth of the oven where they sampled bread, drank wine, and talked of the Old Country they left behind.

Further up the block, close to Danny's Pool Room was the storefront occupied by a Gypsy family consisting of a mother and her two adult children. Maria ran a small business selling trinkets, inexpensive jewelry, and offered Tarot card readings with her daughter Isabella. Her son Joseph was a talented violinist and gave lessons to young and old interested in learning the instrument. As the result of indifference exhibited by many neighborhood residents, the family members were aloof and leary of people's motives. It was no different back in Italy where Gypsies were treated with disdain and not trusted.

Mary, Isabella, and Joseph had resided in Brooklyn for a number of years but were still not entirely accepted. This would all change come one frigid December day when Joseph was on his way home after giving a lesson. He walked briskly with his violin tucked under his arm and his hands shoved in his pockets for warmth. He wasn't far from home when he heard a startling cry for help. He immediately stopped in his tracks and looked around to determine its source. Joseph heard it again and realized it was a woman. He then noticed a column of smoke rising from a nearby house and sirens of fire trucks in the background. Without forethought, he ran up the front steps and set his violin down. He tried the door and was relieved when it opened, but he was met with a wall of smoke as the screams grew louder and more frantic. He was able to determine that they were coming from the second level.

He covered his nose and mouth with his handkerchief and bounded upstairs. This time he was greeted with flames. The fire was to his right and the screaming to his left. He rushed through a half-open door and saw a woman lying on the floor. He reached down to help the now half-conscious woman who had an injured leg. He knew he had little time before the fire would engulf the both of them. Without hesitation, he lifted her up and carried her into the smoke-filled hallway and down the flight of steps. They met two firemen at the front door who helped them outside to safety and fresh air. A number of onlookers had gathered on the sidewalk, and they burst into applause and cheers when they saw Joseph and the woman appear relatively unharmed.

The firemen later informed everyone that if it not for the unselfish and brave actions of the young man, the outcome would have been tragic. The local people were so grateful to Joseph that he and his family were recipients of food and gifts in appreciation for his unselfish deed. The once undeservedly shunned family received their just restitution through an act of unconditional mercy.

Under the Stars

It was the last week of August, and the boys were feeling down about the end of summer and the return of teachers and homework. They wanted to do something that wouldn't be possible during the school year. The gang sat in the shade of a large tree in front of Joey's house and contemplated their dilemma. Suggestions were presented and nixed due to reluctance to repeat the same old thing. "I guess we're gonna do the same old stuff. It's no use," Bach whined with boredom. The others remained silent in agreement.

"Wait a minute," Dominick said, perking up, "I have an idea. The big empty lot between Red's and Bach's is the perfect place to camp out. There are a few trees and enough rocks to make a fire pit in the back."

"And then what?" Bach questioned.

"We can sleep out, and since it's so close to all our houses, our mothers might not mind," Dominick added.

"And it's not supposed to rain the next few days, and we can sleep under the stars next to a fire. Wow!" Red chimed in enthusiastically.

"Boy, that'll be really neat!" Goose said.

"I don't know," Joey said cautiously, "my mother's pretty strict with me because I'm the youngest."

"If that's the case, then ask one of your older brothers to camp out with us, too," Red suggested.

"Yeah, I'll betcha my brother will come, too," Henry stated hopefully.

"Let's do it tomorrow night," Dominick proposed. "We'll have tonight to work on our mothers."

"And tomorrow during the day we can set up the camp," Bach interjected with excitement.

"It's better to eat supper with our families before we meet up," instructed Red, "and if anyone wants to bring a potato to roast in the coals, it will be even better."

That night, all the boys used their best diplomacy to persuade their parents to allow them to carry out their plans. The greatest advantage the boys had was the proximity of the vacant lot. It was close enough that any family member could check on them at any time.

When the boys met the next day to set up, they were glad to hear that all their families were in support. Their immediate attention would be preparing the camp site. The six young men vigorously began to clear debris away from the back of the lot. After raking a section clean, they gathered rocks and built a circular fire pit. The soil there was soft and loamy which made digging easy. It consequently made sitting or lying down much more comfortable.

By late afternoon the site was completed to the boys' satisfaction. They hung around and talked about their upcoming night's venture and agreed to meet there at 7:30, providing all went well.

As the hour approached, Bach and Red were the first to show up since the site was not far from the rear windows of their houses. Each of the boys brought a blanket, and Bach was able to bring his father's canvas knapsack. They sat down on short logs which encircled the fire pit, and the two friends talked about neighborhood gossip as they waited for the others to show up.

Dominick, after having eaten supper, left his house and was relieved that his mother hadn't reneged. He had a rolled-up blanket under his arm and a burlap bag filled with things he might use. A few houses along the way, he met up with Joey and his older brother Mike, and they all headed toward the empty lot. When they arrived, they saw that Henry was already seated alongside Bach and Red. The only person missing was Goose.

Everyone picked out places to bed down for the night. Bach passed around an army entrenching shovel to dig out depressions in the soil so they could conform to their individual contours making the ground more comfortable.

They all heard a loud voice coming from the street just as they settled around the fire pit. It was Goose hurrying toward them. "Hey you guys, I'm a little late, but I made it.

Did I miss anything?" Goose said breathlessly as he flung a duffle bag from his shoulder. Everyone laughed at their likeable, rambunctious friend.

"Goose, believe me," Dominick responded, "you didn't miss anything."

"What did you bring, the kitchen sink?" chided Red. "The bag looks heavier than you."

"Nah, just a few things I might need," Goose defended. He proceeded to dump out the contents. Out dropped an axe, a saw, a canteen, six cans of beans with a can opener, an army sleeping bag and a pillow. His friends shook their heads in amazement.

"Are you sure you didn't forget anything?" Bach asked, rolling his eyes.

"If you think I did, I'll go home and get it," Goose said with seriousness.

"I'm only kidding, you big dope!" Bach said with a loud laugh.

"Well, Goose," Dominick interjected, "if anybody forgot somethin', we know you have it." The others chuckled.

As twilight set in, Red lit a fire as the others gathered around. They soon realized they would need more wood if they wanted the fire to last through the night. Dominick, Goose, and a few others volunteered to scavenge the neighborhood for any discarded wood, since they were not in the middle of the woods with no available trees to chop down.

In a short time, each returned with wooden crates and pieces of scrap lumber. Not to be outdone, Goose dragged back two heavy wooden pallets and seemingly hit the jackpot. With the added supply of scrap wood combined with what they had already was more than enough to last through the night.

Some of the boys brought potatoes from home and were anxious to bury them in the coals of the fire once the flames died down. Not far from the camp site was a puddle which was exactly what they needed. They scooped up the mud and covered the potatoes before they stuck them inside the embers to bake. A half hour later they removed them from the crimson coals and cracked open the mud casings to reveal the steaming hot potatoes. They all had eaten supper, but somehow were hungry once again. Joey and Mike brought six frankfurters and skewered them on green saplings to roast over the fire.

An hour later, after everyone was stuffed, the boys began to settle down and prepare their spot where they chose to sleep. The bedrolls were positioned around the fire. One by one, the tired boys gave in to slumber and the night, except the ever-vigilant Goose. It didn't take long for him to notice a shadow on the side of Bach's house. He took a second glance and yelled, "Look! A mountain lion!" The others sat up to see what he was talking about and saw a shadowy image. Red sprang to his feet, as did Dominick. Everyone's eyes were glued to the slow-moving creature. Suddenly, to all their relief, they heard a meow. It was Rocky, a neighborhood tomcat passing in front of the fire and casting a huge shadow on the side of the house. In relief, they all laughed.

"Leave it to you, Goose," Dominick said, "to think it was a mountain lion and in Brooklyn!"

"I wasn't taking any chances," defended Goose.

Everyone returned to their places by the fire but continued to tease Goose. Twenty minutes later, Dominick felt something moist touch his cheek as he gazed at the stars on his back. He was about to jump to his feet when he realized it was his dog Prince. Dominick reached out to pet him as Prince nuzzled him affectionately. The dog made himself comfortable by stretching alongside him and resting his chin on Dominick's stomach. Prince apparently decided to spend the night. The boy was happy to have his protector by his side.

An hour later, unbeknownst to the kids, Red's father quietly approached the camp. Seeing that everything was okay, he quietly went back home. Not long afterward, the boys had another concerned adult who wanted to check on them. It was Dominick's brother Jimmy who was sent out by Carolina to have a look. He tiptoed closer and could see by the fire light and the sounds of the sleeping boys that everything was fine. Jimmy turned and walked away shaking his head and smiling. In the background, a low, clanging sound of a trolley car faded away into the night.

Unforgettable Characters

The Human Telegraph

Lucy was a colorful local woman and friend to everyone who played an integral role in the neighborhood. She had an uncanny ability to be at the exact location where any embarrassing altercation might take place. At the least, she would always be present to overhear gossip, whether true or not. This information was quickly dispatched to anyone who would listen as she made her daily rounds along her itinerary of four or five blocks. For example, if a husband stopped at a bar after work his wife would know before he arrived home. God forbid she should see a man or a woman talking to the opposite sex; everyone on the block would know about it instantly. It was amazing how normal, everyday activities could be blown out of proportion.

Lucy worked for her two sons who were bookmakers, and she was entrusted to carrying the number slips. This worked out well, for who would have ever thought that this innocent-looking Italian mother was a runner for numbers? Dressed in an oversized, pocketed sweater and her husband's shoes, she had a unique appearance. She was gregarious but also a very shrewd woman.

Husbands and children in the neighborhood disliked her vehemently and tried to avoid running into her. Lucy, though, had another side to her. She could be very compassionate and generous; she was first to offer assistance if anyone or a family needed help. This stemmed from her upbringing in a harsh, dirt-poor town in southern Italy where the only way to survive was to help each other. All and all, she was a good-hearted friend to have, regardless of idiosyncrasies. So it was not a surprise that she was godmother to Dominick and his brother Frank. Therefore, Lucy was known to the Donato family as *comare Lucia*.

When she stopped by for a visit, which could be at any time, she had an unorthodox way of entering. She would immediately open the door before knocking and then once inside, announce herself with a bang on the door, "I'm here!" Carolina and Rose were especially happy and amused by her visits, for it was an opportunity for them to hear the latest gossip in the neighborhood. Lucy displayed great affection to Carolina and her children, and more than once proved she was a good and dependable friend with a most unique personality.

Cop on the Beat

'Clancey', an Irish policeman who patrolled the neighborhood was the only representative of authority. His words were the law, and his opinion had great influence. One had to admire his audacity and bravery. He had a preconceived idea that most Italians were no accounts and mafia. So when Clancey appeared in the neighborhood, he was entering into enemy territory. His mere presence was especially an irritant to all malcontents. Dice and card games quickly ended at the initial sight of him. Brandishing his night stick, Clancey thought nothing of scattering a gang of street thugs. His prowess with the club had been demonstrated many times. If a culprit attempted to run, Clancey would toss the stick so it would bounce along the sidewalk or cobblestone street until it hit the back of the legs or knees of the culprit, bringing him down.

There were times when young Italian boys would taunt the Irish policeman until he had to chase after them, which ended most times with futile results. Dominick and other local neighborhood kids were always playing tricks on him; when they would spot him coming, they would be prepared to execute some prank that would embarrass him. They were very inventive in their schemes.

One summer day in 1922, Clancey was making his usual rounds, and Bach came up with a mischievous idea. Every afternoon when the temperature was hot, the policeman would stop at a sweet shop and buy an ice cream cone. He would walk outside and sit on a small stone wall near the open lot where the Regerrios had their vegetable garden. Clancey would routinely sit with his back to the garden and watch the street in front of him. Bach told the others where the garden hose was located, and the boys smiled as they surmised Bach's intention.

Predictably, Clancey sat down to enjoy his ice cream as Red and Dominick uncoiled the hose within his range. They waited until the perspiring cop made himself comfortable and crossed his legs to relax. Red signaled Bach to turn on the water. Dominick manned the hose at the unsuspecting officer of law, and within seconds, the garden hose stiffened with water as he aimed at Clancey's back. A strong, cold burst came through the nozzle; the heavy stream saturated the target. It almost knocked him off the wall where he was sitting, and he immediately jumped to his feet. Soaked from his hat to his shoes, Clancey stood motionless for a few seconds and then turned around with a barrage of profanity. He insulted the heritage of the culprits and their families. Dominick dropped the hose as he and Red hid behind the shed and doubled over with laughter. Thoroughly drenched, Clancey was a sight. Passersby looked over their shoulders at the irate policeman, afraid to smile at his misfortune. By the time he realized what had happened and who the perpetrators were, the guilty boys had run off stumbling with laughter.

Clancey, in desperation, finally gave up and threw his arms in the air, water squishing out from his shoes as he walked away.

The Violin Maestro

At the center of the block was an eccentric master violin teacher. He had performed with symphony orchestras in both his native country of Italy and in the United States. Umberto was a caricature, from his pencil-thin mustache to his large, fluffy ribbon bowtie. He was a fine teacher, and wealthy people in fancy cars would drive into the neighborhood for their children's lessons. Though the flamboyant musician was well-liked and respected by most, the sounds of students' strained notes resounded from his studio and were not appreciated by many of his neighbors. Umberto truly wanted to have the neighborhood kids to take the opportunity to learn and appreciate classical music. He genuinely desired to lift young people out of their harsh existence to a higher, finer level. The majority of the local boys ridiculed the way he dressed and spoke and did not understand his ways at all.

One fourth of July, Dominick and the rest of the gang were setting off firecrackers in celebration when they decided to have some fun with Umberto. The violin teacher was instructing a young boy in his musical scales. The musician routinely went to the open window and yelled at the boys on the street to be quieter. This did not go too well with them, and they began to plot a way of getting back at him for his reprimanding. Red looked at Dominick and said, "Let's get even with the fancy Maestro." Dominick agreed.

"Red, do you have any firecrackers left?" he asked. "I already blew up the ones I had."

"Yeah, Dom, I have two left."

"Okay. Let's climb the tree near his window and toss them in," Dominick suggested.

"Sounds good to me," Red responded with mischievous glee.

The two boys silently climbed up the tree to a place where a branch was level with Umberto's open window. Inside, a little Fauntleroy-type with a Dutch boy haircut was seriously making awful, screeching noises on his violin. It was so irritating that the cats and dogs on that side of the street were running for cover from the ear-piercing sounds. Dominick and Red decided this would be the ideal time to strike.

They lit the short fuses and threw the two firecrackers inside. The first explosive was surprisingly loud followed by people scurrying out of harm's way. A moment later, the blast of the second firecracker erupted. This time the boys heard shrieking and Umberto cursing the unseen culprits. Dominick and Red quickly scurried down and almost fell out of the tree with laughter.

When their feet hit the ground, they took off running, and when they looked back, they saw a red cushion fly out of the window followed by a shoe. The Maestro leaned out the window, and in a rage of profanity, shouted at the two, escaping troublemakers.

The Returning Hobo

One of the most intriguing personalities to frequent the neighborhood was a middle-aged man known as Clyde. He would show up on the block every summer's end sometime between August and September. He had a circular itinerary which brought him to the southern and western states in the winter and northward again in the summer. He was a free spirit who moved about the states on freight trains. He would hop rides on cargo and cattle cars, and like many others, made this his life's vocation.

Clyde would arrive in small towns and work a couple of weeks picking vegetables or helping to mend fences and fix barns. He usually stayed and worked on the same farms every year. The farmers and ranchers looked forward to him helping them during his annual trek.

When Clyde would arrive in Brooklyn late August, the store owners and tradesmen would hire him usually for a month or so. The neighborhood boys awaited his arrival every year with happy anticipation. After his work, he would stroll down the streets in the evening and meet up with familiar faces and engage in nostalgic conversations. At this time after supper, the boys would catch up with Clyde and enjoyed hearing of the many places and things he encountered on his journey through the states. They found him fascinating as well as his free, easy, and uncluttered lifestyle. They, too, dreamed of hopping a train and leaving the city streets behind. Clyde's persona attracted a lot of attention; most of the locals admired him but were afraid to admit it for fear of public criticism. On the other hand, the young people envied his carefree ways. Bach and Red in particular, always dreamed of going out west, and the idea of just hitching a ride on a train was enticing.

When Clyde was in town, he was usually surrounded by a number of neighborhood kids. The fathers and mothers were not enamored by his presence, for he represented rebellious ideas. The talk of dropping everything and going out west to work on a cattle ranch was too appealing to the ears of their offspring. But sadly, for the kids, Clyde did not remain long enough. Regretfully, when he did leave, the absence of his dynamic presence was felt by all, whether they admitted it or not.

The Bumbling Thieves

Among the everyday hardworking people was an element of shady good-for-nothings. They were not above taking advantage of any and every opportunity to cheat or rob. Some were so criminally-minded that their own families were ashamed to be related to them. Three friends were such an example, involved in petty crimes. The trio—Augie, Lenny, and Rocky—were smart enough to do their evil deeds outside the boundaries of the neighborhood. If they scored big, they couldn't help but boast. When they were successful, it was not uncommon to see the three strutting along the street sporting expensive clothes and smoking Cuban cigars. They were comical characters and seemed impervious to condemnation and judgmental stares. After hijacking trucks, there were occasions when they would bring the contraband back to the neighborhood to sell. Most of the time, people would just look the other way because they could buy items for pennies on the dollar. It would end badly if any righteous person thought of turning in the thieves to the police. Fear of physical injury perpetuated the trio's criminal behavior and secured a safe haven.

Once a month, racks of new clothes—men's and women's—would appear on the sidewalks for sale. This cache of high-end clothing did not last long, as the so-called honest people snatched them up without blinking an eye. The origin of the low-priced fancy goods never crossed the buyer's conscience. Bottles of costly perfume, coats, and bourbon, rye, and champagne would also be offered for sale. The most recently stolen goods would appear immediately on the streets.

Augie, Lenny, and Rocky were involved in an episode which became a legendary neighborhood story. One late afternoon, Dominick, Bach, Red, and Goose had been playing cards in front of the sweet shop and were about to go home when they saw Augie's car pull up. It was moving slowly toward them but something wasn't right. As it approached them, it was obvious that it had been in an accident. Somehow, the roof and the sides of the car were dented. It finally clinked alongside the curb close to the boys. Lenny—smiling and shaking his head—was the first to exit the car. A moment later, Augie and Rocky emerged laughing and nodding in disbelief. The kids wondered what could be so amusing about their damaged vehicle. A passerby who knew the trio well stopped and asked them, "What's so funny, Augie?"

"You wouldn't believe it. You wouldn't even see it in a movie!" Augie answered, and then continued in a long-winded explanation. "We drive up toward Tarrytown and then wanna take a road off the main highway. We end up in a small, dinky town with a post office, general store, and a bank. Rocky looks at me and Lenny and says 'we can't let this chance go by. We're in a one-horse town with no cops. Let's knock off the bank.' So I look at Lenny and we say, 'yeah, let's do it.' I have my 38 pistol, and Rocky's got a 45, and we walk in." Augie paused to drag on his cigarette. "The place is empty, only two jamoke tellers. I says to myself, 'I must be dreamin'. This is too easy.' So we go ahead and clean out the money drawers. The big vault was already locked and the timer was set, so we settle for what was in the drawers. It's only about a thousand bucks. This is like stealin' from a baby, so we take it. We leave the two jamokes and take off. We're all happy—we have a thousand bucks for spending. We get on the open road and gun it. All of a sudden, we see a car in the rear view mirror comin' up on us. I push the gas pedal to the floor but we're not losin' 'em. I get up to 85 MPH and we're stayin' just ahead 'em." Augie talked with his hands, flaying his arms dramatically. "I's still see them in the mirror. Then we go into a curve but I'm goin' too fast. Then I lose control and before we know it, we're flippin'. Over and over! I'm thinkin' we're all gonna die. We're tumbling hard down the hill. Then don't ask me how, the car stops dead. I bang my head a few times, but I'm okay.

Lenny over here hurts his shoulder, but no big deal." Augie laughed at the ridiculous tale. "Lenny and I look in the back to see how Rocky is. He ain't movin'. We think he's dead. I shake 'em and he groans. In a minute, he's awake and saying his ribs hurt. That's all! Then I take a good look out and see that we landed upright on the tires. I says, 'you gotta be kiddin'! We're on the road under the one we was on!' Then I says, 'this has gotta be a miracle!' I step on the gas and we're movin'. I look up to the other road where we was and I see the cops standin' by their car and scratching their heads lookin' down on us. So I get up to 45 MPH but it won't go faster. But we're movin'." By now, the poor passerby was rolling his eyes and wondering when Augie would stop talking. "I figure I start takin' all the back roads in case we're being followed but nobody was behind us. So we just take our sweet time and drive south to the city. Pretty soon, we're over the Brooklyn Bridge and home. We must be the luckiest dumb asses alive!"

The beaten-up car with its mud-splattered roof and dents became the joke and the talk of the neighborhood for a long time to come.

The Big Game

During the spring and summer months, the St. John's home baseball team would play against any local team good enough to go up against them. They had a reputation for being one of the best teams in Brooklyn, and they let everyone know it. The many games on their schedule usually resulted with them being defeated only once or twice. The challenge was open to any team between the ages fourteen and eighteen who could muster the talent. These confident, cocky ball players had taken on adult teams and defeated them also. In the beginning of July, the neighborhood teenage boys would play ball as they always had in the past. So one afternoon as they walked to the open lot, Bach came up with a bright idea. He suggested they get together with some of the older guys and play St. John's. His friends looked him and asked,

"Have you been drinking too much of your father's wine?" and laughed.

"Wait a minute. Let's think about it a little more. Maybe it's not so crazy," Red said.

"We do have older brothers," added Dominick. "And if we could get them to join us, we might have a chance to beat them."

"You know how much the guys from the neighborhood hate St. John's. If our brothers thought we could beat those big mouths, I think they would join us," Danny added.

In the following weeks the guys practiced every chance they could, at least once and sometimes even twice a day. In the meantime, they all approached their older brothers and other friends about the idea. At first, their siblings thought it was nuts based on St. John's reputation. But all thought it would be a great opportunity to beat the pants off them. The unifying factor was their dislike for the bully team. A few other kids in particular wanted to recruit anyone who would make the team credible. One was Carmen, Goose's seventeen-year-old cousin. He was strong and could hit a ball a mile. During that past year in gym class, he hit a ball that reached a four hundred foot fence in one bounce. The coach had a fit because Carmen had no interest in playing on the varsity baseball team. The other prospect they wanted badly was Eddie Hurley, an Irish kid who could throw a wicked fastball. He was Bach's cousin who lived two blocks away. This sixteen year old would spend a lot of his idle time throwing a ball or a rock through a mounted barrel hoop in empty lots. Fortunately, for the neighborhood guys, Eddie jumped at the chance to join them.

The next position they had to fill was that of catcher, the most difficult because good ones were rare. One of Red's friends knew of one who had just moved from Chicago. The guy had caught ball for an adult team, even though he was only seventeen. Red was a very good talker, and it only took Red only one meeting to convince the newcomer to get on board. His name was Tommy Schultz, and he was thrilled at the opportunity to play on a new team.

Within a few days, they all met up at the large open lot on the corner of Troy and Prospect Pl. to begin practice. In the hard soil they scratched out a pitcher's mound and home plate. Then they paced off and marked first, second, and third base. Tommy emptied a burlap bag containing his catcher's glove, mask, chest protector, and shin guards. In a few moments, he had his gear on, and Eddie took the cue and started throwing. The rest of the guys took turns throwing and hitting balls to each other. This went on for an hour before they designated who would play what position. They decided that Carmen would be at first base, Danny at second. Red would be shortstop, and third base would be Bach. In the outfield in left would be Joey, Dominick in center, and Goose in right. There were also two substitutes in case someone got injured. One was Henry, Red's younger brother, and Carl, Dominick's younger brother. Both of them had played since they could first pick up a bat and ball.

This band of ambitious young men had little over a

month and a half to get into competitive shape and practiced seriously every day. At times, though, it wasn't possible for everyone to assemble. When that was the case four, five, or six would show up and do the best they could.

Ten days before they were going to play St. John's, the guys wanted to get a good idea of how good they were and challenged an adult team from a nearby neighborhood. When the more seasoned team heard who had wanted to play them, they were all amused but agreed to play the match-up. If anything, this team would teach the younger guys a lesson or two. Dominic, Red, and the other kids were excited to have a chance to play the more experienced team.

The date was set, and that Sunday they met the other team at a ball field less than a mile away. Their opponents were already waiting when the neighborhood boys arrived. This time the rookies would play on a field with real base pads and an actual home plate and pitcher's mound. The waiting team greeted them, and they all shook hands. The captain of the opposing team asked Red and the others if they wanted to bat first. Red looked at his teammates and declined the offer, and they soon took to the field. Eddie tossed a few warm-up pitches to Tommy, and to the surprise of the adult team, Eddie's throws were so hard that they made a sharp sound as the ball hit Tommy's glove. Some looked at each other and shook their heads with surprise. Spectators gathered and stood or sat on the ground in anticipation of the start of the game. The first batter up approached the plate. There were two umpires to call the game, one behind home plate and the other behind second base. Eddie waited for the first batter to get ready then crouched. He looked at Tommy and fired the ball. It went straight down the middle of the plate as it passed the batter. It was a strike. The batter got settled again and waited for the next pitch. *Swoosh*, the ball whizzed by as the batter swung and only hit the air. Strike two. The hitter again steadied himself and waited for the third pitch. Eddie locked eyes on Tommy's sign and then let go. This time he threw an inside curveball. The batter was obviously waiting for a fastball like the other two and swung too soon in anticipation of it. He missed the ball by half a foot and was out on three pitches.

The next hitter stepped up and got into position to receive his first pitch. Eddie leaned back, and out of his crouch, fired a sizzling fastball right past him waist high. Strike one. The batter got ready once again, and this time Eddie tossed a curveball, and the batter caught a piece of it, fowling it off to the right. The batter positioned himself yet again. Eddie straightened up and threw a fastball knee high. The batter swung and missed. Strike three.

The third batter fidgeted and then waited. Eddie hurled the ball down the middle as the hitter fowled it off behind the catcher and into the spectators. Strike one. The batter waited for the next pitch as Eddie threw this one side-arm. The batter swung a little too late and popped it straight up as Carmen at first base made an easy catch of it. Third out, side was retired.

Now it would be the neighborhood guys batting in the

bottom of the inning. First up was Red, and he wasted no time getting ready. The opposing pitcher leaned back and threw a wicked fastball right past him waist high. Strike one. Red quickly got into position and waited. The pitcher delivered another fastball, and this time, Red slammed a line drive right at the short stop who caught it easily.

Next up was Dominick. The lanky pitcher threw an outside curveball chest high. Dominick hit straight back at the mound. The hurler threw his glove up to protect his face and caught the drive. Second out.

Bach was the next hitter, and he settled confidently into position and waited. Once again the pitcher wound up and threw the ball hard past the hitter. Strike one. Bach stepped back and repositioned himself for the next pitch. The pitcher wasted no time and threw a belt-high outside curveball. Bach swung and hit it flush, straight over second base for a single. There were two outs; Bach was on first and Carmen was the next hitter. The big guy stepped up and held the bat high as he waited for his first pitch. It was a low and away fastball. Ball one. Carmen stayed put and let it go by. The next pitch was high and inside of which he laid off. Ball two. The third pitch was low and inside. Ball three and no strikes. On the next throw, the pitcher had to either walk him or throw a not-so-hittable pitch to get him to swing wildly. The pitcher decided and threw a chest-high outside pitch which Carmen hit hard to the opposing field, way over the first baseman and continuing over the right fielder's head. The hard-hit ball landed almost a hundred feet beyond the right fielder and rolled further away. Bach took off from first when the ball was hit and easily rounded second and third and reached home plate safely. Meanwhile, Carmen followed close behind Bach around the base pads and headed for home while the throw was being relayed from the outfield. But it was too late as Carmen crossed home plate way ahead of the throw. His happy neighborhood teammates surrounded him enthusiastically. This wasn't what the older, opposing team ever expected.

The following batter was Joey, who popped up the first pitch into the infield which was caught easily and ended the inning.

The next seven innings became a pitcher's duel; the opposing pitcher didn't give up another hit after Carmen's homerun in the first. Meanwhile, Eddie gave up a single in the third, a double in the fifth, and a bunt single in the seventh. But there were no runs scored on any of the hits.

It was the top of the eighth, and Eddie easily struck out the first batter. The second hitter grounded to short an easy out. It was now two outs, and the third batter came to the plate. Eddie got behind with three balls and only one strike. Eddie threw the next pitch which was another sizzling fastball. This time the batter anticipated it and hit the ball solid. The ball came off the bat like a rocket, flying twenty feet over Dominick's head in center field. It was a tremendous blast, and by the time Dominick was able to get to the ball, the batter was already rounding third and heading for home. Dominick threw the ball to the second baseman who relayed the throw home, but it was too late. The fourth batter got up and lined the first pitch to third which Bach caught easily for the third out. The score was two to one in favor of the neighborhood boys.

The bottom of the eighth was brief as Joey fouled out, Bach struck out, and Goose lined out. It was now the crucial top of the ninth. The first opposing batter got into position and waited for the first pitch. Eddie paused a little then threw a breaking curveball that the batter got a good piece of and sent the ball over second for a single. One could see Eddie was upset with himself as he walked around the pitcher's mound to cool off. He calmed down as the next hitter waited. Eddie wasted little time and fired a fast ball belt high past him for a strike. The batter wasn't fazed any as he quickly readied himself for the second pitch. Eddie again wound up and threw another fastball low around the knees as the batter swung and missed. The hitter then waited for the next pitch. Once again Eddie threw his rocket-fast ball, and the batter connected hitting a line drive bullet to third. Bach stuck out his glove, caught the ball midair and swiftly threw to second where Danny tagged the advancing runner from first for a double play and the second out. This took a lot of pressure off of Eddie as he prepared for the third hitter. It was obvious the batter was a little nervous, for it was all up to him. Eddie was anxious to get the game over with as the batter waited for his first pitch. Eddie kicked extra high in his wind-up and released a fastball just above the knees. The batter swung but was too late to hit it. Strike one. The batter got set for the second pitch and this one rocketed past him chest high. Strike two.

Upset with himself, the batter got back into position and waited. Eddie quickly went into his wind-up and again kicked high. The batter was prepared for Eddie's super fastball, but Eddie threw a change up and the hitter over swung and missed the ball by half a foot. Strike three, game over.

This ending was not anticipated, and the neighborhood boys exuberantly swarmed around Eddie. The opposing older and experienced players left shaking their heads in disbelief and even before the celebrating boys could return home, the good news had already spread.

This victory gave the young players a sense of confidence which they would need when they would meet the St. John's team the following week. After celebrating and patting themselves on the back, they all realized they had to knuckle down and prepare for the up and coming big game.

When Monday rolled around, the guys all met at the field at Troy and Prospect and began honing their throwing and catching skills. On the lighter side, some comical criticism about Eddie's throwing circulated. It wasn't entirely a joke; Eddie threw so hard that Tommy's hand was sore after only fifteen minutes of catching. Another minor problem was Carmen; he was hitting the balls so far they were getting lost, and balls were not cheap. The guys joked that they wanted to paint them red so they would be easier to find. Carmen laughed. "Do you want me to hit the long ball or not?"

They all practiced diligently as the days passed quickly. By that Friday, the boys were anxious. After the last day of practice on Saturday, they were as ready as they would ever be for the big game the next day.

At one o'clock on Sunday afternoon, they gathered at the corner and then walked the block to the athletic field across from St. John's Home. When they arrived, the St. John's team was already warming up. The neighborhood team went to another section of the field and did likewise. At one thirty, the two officiating umpires signaled the two teams that the game was about to begin. St. John's looked sharp in their white uniforms and blue lettering. The guys, to the amusement of the opposing players, donned only their street clothes. The St. John's team had half a dozen back-up players as substitutes. The boys had only two extra players—Carl and Henry. Because it was their home field, St. John's had the advantage of being at bat at the bottom of the inning. The looks from the uniformed players said it all. They scorned and ridiculed the appearance of the neighborhood players, and totally dismissed any threat from a team composed of street urchins.

Cocky St. John's took to the field to begin the game. Red was the first batter up. He got into position as the opposing pitcher wasted no time. He wound up and delivered a fastball straight down the middle of the plate. Strike one. Unfazed, Red was ready for the next pitch, and again, a fastball whizzed by just above the knees. Strike two. This time, Red stepped back then returned to the batter's box for the third pitch. The pitcher wound up and threw a hard curving ball which Red swung at and missed. Strike three, one out.

Dominick then stepped up and waited for the pitcher who threw a fastball. Dominick hit it hard, but it was right to the shortstop who caught it; it was the second out.

Bach got up for his turn, held the bat high, and waited. The pitcher kicked high and threw a hard curveball which Bach missed by a mile. Strike one. Bach got himself together and waited for the next pitch. It was a fastball waist-high, and Bach couldn't resist it. He swung, only getting a piece of it as it popped up and was caught by the first baseman. Third out.

The boys then took to the field. Eddie took a few warm-up pitches then Tommy threw the ball around the infield as the first St. John's batter approached the plate. The hitter looked toward Eddie on the mound and stepped into position and waited. Eddie crouched, looked at Tommy for a sign and went into his wind-up. Kicking high, Tommy let go a steaming fastball down the middle of the plate for a strike. The batter took a stretch with the bat behind his back. He stepped into the batter's box again and waited. Eddie went through his usual form and fired a rocket ball waist high. Second strike. Unaffected, the hitter got ready for the next pitch and held his bat with anticipation. This throw was even faster. By the time he swung, the ball had already reached the catcher's glove for the third strike. He walked away cursing under his breath.

The next batter was a little smaller in height. He didn't have to wait long. Eddie fired a fastball. The batter swung hard, and the ball was fouled off along the third base line. Again, the batter poised himself as Eddie let go another sizzling fastball chest-high over the plate, right past the batter. Strike two. The batter had no choice but to wait for the next pitch. From his high kick, Eddie threw a curve which broke to the outside. The hitter had expected another fastball and missed it. Second out.

The third batter was St. John's wiry first baseman. He fidgeted for a while then got ready. Eddie waved off a sign from Tommy and decided to throw a fastball which the hitter laid off. It was a strike. He held the bat up and waited. Eddie then delivered his throw in the same exact spot, only faster. The batter swung and missed. Strike two. A little overwhelmed, he got in position for the next throw. Eddie wasted little time and fired a speeding curveball which the batter hit a little late and popped it up straight between home and first. Carmen got under it and caught the ball for the last out of the inning.

The first inning set the mood for the rest of the game. It was a very close pitcher's contest, as no runs were scored by either side. Eddie had only given up two singles, one in the fourth and one in the fifth inning. St. John's pitcher allowed a double in the fifth and a single in the sixth.

Bach was the first batter at the top of the seventh inning, and it looked like another fruitless opportunity. Bach had two strikes on him and a ball. The St. John's pitcher threw a curve which Bach tagged for a single over first base. Carmen was up next, and the pitcher threw some bad pitches, as he did not want to give him anything good to hit. Carmen had three balls and one strike. The pitcher was then forced to throw him a decent pitch. He didn't want another runner on the bases with no outs. Looking at the batter, the pitcher then leaned back and threw a fastball. Carmen anticipated a fastball and swung a little early but was able to get under the ball and lift it to centerfield and over the fielder's head. The crowd cheered. Bach took off, raced around second, then past third and was waved home which he easily made. Meanwhile, Carmen's hit was so long, he was able to make it to third base. Next up was Joey who took the first pitch for a strike. He quickly recovered and waited for the next pitch. The St. John's pitcher wound up and threw a fastball which Joey managed to hit, but it went straight at the pitcher who gloved it for the first out.

Danny was up next and took the first pitch for a ball. Digging in, he waited as the pitcher delivered an outside fastball which Danny hit a ground ball at the shortstop who paused as he held Carmen at third but threw out Danny at first for the second out.

Goose stepped up to bat. It was obvious that the pitcher was in a hurry to throw. His first pitch was so close, it brushed Goose's shirt as it sped by. Ball one. Goose stepped back and settled himself. The next pitch was a fastball that Goose connected and drove straight at the pitcher who was able to knock the ball down but held Carmen at third. The pitcher quickly fired the ball to first and eliminated Goose. Third out, inning over, one run scored for the boys.

Bottom of the seventh and St. John's was behind by one run. The first batter up hit Eddie's first pitch straight to short where Red scooped it up and threw the runner out at first. Second batter got two pitches that were balls. Eddie threw three consecutive strikes to get him out as the crowd roared.

171

The third batter approached and was visibly mad. The first pitch was a strike above his knees. The second pitch came in waist high, which he swung at too late and missed. He stood and waited for the third pitch. It was a curveball which he hit to leftfield which Joey caught easily. Inning over, no runs.

Tommy was the first batter up at the top of the eighth inning. The first pitch was too wide for a ball. The second was a fastball down the middle which zipped right by him, and he just looked at it fly by. Tommy got set again and waited for the pitcher to throw another hard fastball, but this time Tommy got his bat around quickly enough to meet the ball solid. The ball flew in the air thirty feet between the leftfielder and the centerfielder. Tommy took off like a shot and passed first and then around second. The ball was still rolling away from the fielders as he sped toward third base, and his teammates waved him home. It was a stand-up homerun as the outfielders had just gotten to the ball. Eddie was up; he hit the first pitch and popped it up into the infield. It was an easy first out.

Red's turn was next, and he approached the plate with bat in hand. He took a ball and then took two strikes. He hit a line drive on the fourth pitch straight at the third baseman who caught it in the air for the second out.

Dominick stepped up, and the first pitch was a strike just above the knees. Next time a fastball came in; he stuck his bat out to bunt but popped the ball toward the pitcher who caught it for the third out. One run scored.

It was now the bottom of the eighth for St. John's. Their big hitter was up first. The first pitch was a high curve for a ball. The next one was a fastball belt high and a strike. The third pitch was another fastball but this time the batter swung and hit the ball toward center. Dominick in center was playing him deep, but he still had to run further back and barely caught the ball. Hurt with a sprained ankle, Dominick walked away limping. He was helped off the field, and his team brought in Carl, Dominick's younger brother, for a substitute.

The next hitter for St. John's jumped on the first pitch and hit it at the pitcher. Eddie raised his glove in front of his face and caught the hard-hit ball for the second out.

The third hitter watched helplessly as the fast curveball whipped across the plate. Determined not to strike out, the batter swung at the third pitch and popped it up behind home plate as Tommy raced under and caught it. The side was out.

It was two to nothing in favor of the neighborhood boys. The St. John's pitcher vowed not to give up another run. Bach was the leadoff batter in the ninth as the pitcher threw a change up pitch which Bach took for a strike. The next pitch was a curve which he drilled into the infield. It took a hard hop, but the shortstop handled it perfectly, throwing Bach out at first.

Carmen stepped up to the plate, held the bat high, and waited. The pitcher didn't hesitate and threw a hard curveball. To everyone's surprise, Carmen jumped on it, hitting it hard and long to centerfield. The St. John's fielder ran deep to his left side, and at the last second, bounded into the air, making a stunning catch for the second out.

Joey was up next. He positioned himself for the first

pitch, and the pitcher wound up, throwing a fastball that was so speedy that Joey could only watch it go by. Joey got ready again, and like the first pitch, the ball rocketed past Joey once more. Strike two. He looked a little forlorn as he waited for the next bullet express. The pitcher went through his big wind-up and threw a change up curve which Joey missed by a foot. It was the last out of the inning. No runs scored.

It was the bottom of the ninth, and it was put up or shut up for St. John's. Their first batter was their first baseman, and he stepped up and waited for Eddie to make the first pitch. Eddie released a searing fastball. The hitter demonstrated lightning-fast reflexes and smacked the ball into leftfield way over Joey's head. The hitter was a speedster, and he sprinted past first and second, and as he came to third, he glanced over his shoulder and realized he would have no problem stretching it into a homerun. As he touched home plate, Joey had just retrieved the ball with no chance to throw him out.

It was now two to one. St. John's needed another run to tie and two runs to win. The next batter stepped up while Eddie was furious with himself for giving up the homerun. He shot an intimidating look at the second batter and released a fastball past the anxious hitter. Strike one. Without hesitation, Eddie followed with two more fastballs and struck out the batter.

Next to bat was the catcher for St. John's. He took the first pitch for a strike and then took an inside pitch for a ball. As the third pitch approached the plate, he swung and hit a hard-lined drive to Danny at short, which he caught easily for the second out. St. John's was down to their last out.

The next hitter nervously got into position. The throw was called a ball, for it missed the corner of the plate. The next pitch was a bullet fastball chest high from which the hitter held off. Strike. The batter paused and then settled in as Eddie went to his fastball once again. It flew toward the batter; he swung and hit it solid. It careened over second base for a single, keeping St. John's alive.

Up next was their best hitter, and it was all up to him to do something. Eddie did not want to give him anything good. So the next two pitches were balls. Eddie decided he must go with his reliable fastball. Out of his wind-up, he threw the ball, and it rocketed toward the plate. The batter correctly anticipated the belt high pitch and connected, slamming the ball deep into right centerfield. Carl immediately began to run in the direction of the ball when he heard the crack of the bat. He miraculously arrived at the precise moment the ball was about to go between himself and Goose who was playing rightfield. In desperation, Carl dove at the ball and caught it, collapsing to the ground. He barely avoided a collision with Goose and somehow managed to hold onto the ball without dropping it. This was the final out of the game. The neighborhood boys defeated the prestigious St. John's and everyone's number one baseball adversary.

News of this victory spread throughout the northern part of Brooklyn, and all the boys returned to the neighborhood and treated as conquering heroes.

Unforeseen

In the early years, when it was just Rose and Jimmy with their parents, the family lived on the poverty-stricken East Side of Manhattan. It was challenging to survive in the densely overcrowded area. Shabby tenements were packed with newly arrived immigrants from all over Europe. Fortunately, Giuseppe had always found work in the busy shoe industry. The family lived on the second floor of a poorly built, pre-Civil War structure. In the rear was a web of clotheslines which spanned above littered alleyways. Clothing of all sorts would hang out to dry and dangle over the narrow spaces. Here children played cheerfully, unconscious of the squalor conditions around them. Little Rose was too small to join in but looked out open windows and envied the other kids having fun below. She was a lively toddler intent on being among the happy bunch. So much so, that one day she managed to pull a chair closer to the window. She stood on it to get a better view of the children playing. She smiled and wished she could be with the older girls jumping rope. To get a better look, she shifted her tiny feet, and as she did, tripped on an untied shoelace and suddenly plummeted out the window. She fell screaming, but miraculously her fall was broken by a clothesline; she bounced off the line and onto the hard ground. In another room, Carolina heard Rose shriek and hurried to the window. She frantically looked out and saw her little girl sprawled on the alley below. Concerned children and adults tried to help.

Someone had brought back a doctor who lived close by and was already tending to Rose when Carolina frantically arrived. The doctor shook his head and said, "If not for that clothesline breaking her fall, she would have been critically injured." As it was, Rose had the wind knocked out of her and was bleeding from a small gash on the side of her head. In a few minutes, to the happy surprise of everyone, the lucky little girl stood up albeit crying. The doctor put an ice pack on the cut which stopped the bleeding and told Carolina that her daughter would be alright. But if she started to suffer from headaches to not waste any time and call on him again. Astonishingly, Rose seemed to be okay in a day or two and quickly resumed being a little girl.

In the ensuing years, the family moved from the populated East Side across the bridge to Brooklyn. The members of the family increased with the births of Tony, Frank, Dominick, and Carl. Rose, aside from her mother, was respected for her opinion regarding household decisions. It was common for her to make sure the boys did their part by doing chores and completing their homework assignments. Therefore, between Rose and older Jimmy, the boys were kept in line. This lifted some of the pressure off their parents. Before long, and almost unnoticed, Rose blossomed into a young woman, and nervous, young men came to call. Her eye was fixed only on Joe, a local suitor who adored her. His kindness and honesty were obvious, for they were demonstrated in his everyday dealings with everyone in the neighborhood. He was a well-respected tradesman who was handsomely paid for his services. Within only a few months, he and Rose found themselves in love, and Joe anxiously asked her to be his wife. She happily accepted his proposal. Giuseppe and Carolina, as well as Rose's brothers from the oldest to the youngest, liked Joe from the start and appreciated his gentle and sincere character. It was easy for them to give the young couple their blessing.

So it was decided that they would be married a year from their engagement. The following weeks were filled with hope and high expectations for Rose and the rest of the family. The anticipation of better times ahead was contagious. Jimmy was also on his way to a new beginning, an important and lucrative career as a regional manager in the shoe business, and Giuseppe was appointed manager of over forty leather shoe craftsmen. At the same time, Dominick was maintaining good grades in a prestigious all-boys high school. Frank was working and finally managing to stay out of trouble. Tony had a good job with a trucking company, driving loads to the major northeastern cities. Times and conditions couldn't have been better.

One ordinary morning, Rose and Carolina prepared breakfast as they had done so many times before; Rose glanced at the clock and exclaimed, "Momma, the time looks a little blurry. I don't think I got enough sleep last night."

"Stop and sit down for a while," advised Carolina, "I'll finish up." Rose took her mother's advice and sat back in the easy chair in the other room. She closed her eyes and relaxed. She dozed off in a few minutes. Twenty minutes later, she was awakened by a noise in the kitchen. Her mother had dropped an empty pot. Rose settled back into her chair and reached over the end table to pick up a magazine. She switched on a lamp to read. As she turned the pages, she realized her eyes were still out of focus. Frightened, she called out to her mother, "Momma, I still cannot see right. I'm scared. What is going on?" Carolina came into the room with concern.

"Maybe you just need eyeglasses. Don't worry so," she said, trying to calm her daughter. Giuseppe, who had just entered the kitchen, was quickly made aware of Rose's situation.

"Figlia mio, don't worry. I will take you to see someone. The doctor is away right now at a convention, but after breakfast, I will take you to see Mr. Shapiro," Giuseppe assured her.

Mr. Shapiro was the local pharmacist who had also gone to medical school. He was an Austrian immigrant, and all who knew him respected his general knowledge in medicine.

They left after breakfast around nine o'clock, and Giuseppe led Rose by the hand. The gracious pharmacist told Rose to have a seat while he took a look at her eyes. After a few minutes, he asked Giuseppe to step into the other room so he could speak to him in private. Giuseppe was instantly alarmed by this but did not show it. Once in the other room, the concerned pharmacist put his hand on Giuseppe's shoulder and continued, "I don't know how to tell you, but I have seen two other people with the same eye condition and they both lost their sight within a year." Giuseppe gasped and then remained quiet as Mr. Shapiro continued, "I'm very sorry, my friend. There is only one person I know who can possibly help her, and he is in Austria and won't be back in New York for a few weeks. He is the best eye specialist in Europe, and he is the only hope. He is very expensive, but it is worth the chance." Giuseppe was numb by the devastating news but told Mr. Shapiro to go ahead and contact the Austrian eye specialist as soon as possible. As far the money was concerned, Giuseppe was sure he could raise it with the help of his sons.

He did not tell Rose about the pharmacist's conclusions, but he did tell her about the eye specialist.

Rose's eyesight was erratic; her eyes were normal on some days, followed by days of blurred vision. It was an extremely depressing and anxious time for Rose. Her world had turned upside down, as well as her family's. The three weeks dragged on, feeling like months until the specialist finally arrived. Because the esteemed eye doctor was good friends with Mr. Shapiro, he arranged to examine Rose at the pharmacy after closing hours. Rose and her parents walked the two short blocks to the drugstore and remained quiet. Upon entering, they met the distinguished and cordial physician who made Rose feel comfortable. He wasted little time and looked at her eyes through half a dozen optic lenses. After fifteen minutes into the examination, the doctor put the instruments back into the case and then took a seat. He remained silent for a time and then said, "I'm afraid that Mr. Shapiro's suspicions of the condition are correct. There is pressure on the optic nerve preventing the normal function of the eyes. This could have been a result by a blow to the head or an injury from a fall many years ago."

Rose and her parents were shocked by the diagnosis; she shook her head in disbelief and remained quiet. As if in a trance, she walked home with Giuseppe and Carolina with no hope on the horizon.

When they arrived home, all the boys were there anxiously awaiting the results, but no one had to say a word; they knew by the expressions that things did not go well. In frustration, Frank slammed the cabinet door, and Tony kicked the wall. Dominick lowered his head in disbelief while Jimmy went over to his sister and hugged her. "Try not to worry. We are all here for you," he whispered, holding back tears. "There is nothing in this world we wouldn't do to help." Rose broke down crying uncontrollably. Her brothers went to her and tried to console her, reinforcing Jimmy's pledge.

Completely decimated, Rose sat down, for she had a lot to assimilate. Her heartbroken parents tried to muster up the energy and acceptance to go on with their mundane activities. In a while, Carolina was in the kitchen trying to busy herself while Giuseppe somberly picked up a newspaper to bury his thoughts. The boys slowly began to resume their normal routines. After a while, a dazed Rose forced a momentary acceptance and went to help her mother in the kitchen.

In the weeks that followed, her vision worsened. Every movement had to be planned to avoid bumping into an open door or wall and stumbling into furniture. It was tremendously depressing to suffer the incremental loss of her sight.

Joe, her fiancé, was beyond supportive and constant. He adored her and encouraged her to endure. He assured her that nothing would change with their plans and relationship. Joe's gracious actions and compassion were endless. Even though Rose knew the extent of his devotion, she did not want Joe to sacrifice so much because of her. This ate away at her until she finally decided to break their engagement. She did not know how to tell him without hurting him.

One evening, Rose invited Joe over to talk. He was very intuitive and surmised something was not right. Rose seemed distant and uneasy. Finally, without hesitation, she said, "I've been seriously thinking about us. Joe, I can't marry you. I will not burden you and have you sacrifice everything for me."

"Rose, please don't say that. I love you so much that

nothing matters. Nothing. The only thing that is important is that we are together," Joe pleaded.

"I know you love me," Rose uttered, tears interrupting her words, "and would do anything...for me. But that is the very...reason...why. You are too good a man to be shackled to me. You need someone who is an equal partner, and you deserve better. I can't let you tie yourself to me. Because I love you and don't want you to be unhappy." Rose paused and then removed the engagement ring from her finger. "Joe, please take this. You will always be my friend and in my heart." With tears in his eyes and his head lowered by the weight of dejection and futility, Joe took the ring and quietly left.

The week that followed was a gloomy one for Rose and the rest of the family. Everyone felt the loss of Joe and his positive presence in their lives. It was so hurtful that no one spoke about it. It was a subject that was avoided, as if Joe never existed. As a result, Rose retreated further into herself and was unusually quiet. At the dinner table, she barely acknowledged those around her. In addition, every day that passed, she was able to see less and less.

Right after eating lunch one day, Rose disappeared into her bedroom. An hour had gone by before Carolina wanted to ask Rose to accompany her to the corner grocery. When she went to open Rose's bedroom door, she found it locked. She then called out to her daughter, but there was no reply. Getting a little concerned, she called out again, this time in a louder tone. Still, no answer. Carolina then summoned Jimmy to come quickly. Dominick had just come in from school when he heard his mother calling out. Sensing urgency, he dropped his books to help. He saw his mother and Jimmy trying to force open Rose's door. Dominick coaxed his mother to stand aside while he and Jimmy put all their weight against it. The lock finally gave way, but the door wasn't budging. Apparently, Rose had moved a heavy piece of furniture against the back of the door. On the third try, the two brothers were able to shove it open. They saw Rose asleep on the bed then heard the hiss and odor of gas. It was sadly evident that Rose had turned the lamp keys on full force and then extinguished the flames. Carolina screamed, knowing that Rose had tried to end her life. Jimmy and Dominick rushed to turn the off the gas and opened the windows. Though unconscious, she was still breathing. Another twenty minutes or so, and she would have succeeded in her intention. They carried Rose into the living room and gently put her on the couch. Carolina fanned her daughter's ashen face to get fresher air into her lungs. In a little while, Rose began to stir and finally regained consciousness. Rose immediately burst into tears and was frantic to realize she had been unsuccessful. "How could you stop me?" she sobbed angrily. "You have no idea how bad it is. I have nothing to live for…nothing! And for heaven's sake, I cannot live with being an anchor around your necks for the rest of my life!"

It was a tragic scene to see her and her distraught family not knowing how to make it better. They did their best to encourage her and help her to see that life was worth living.

It was decided she could not be left alone; a family

member had to be with her twenty-four hours a day. As before, Carolina would spend the day with her. The remainder of the time would be divided into overnight vigils among Giuseppe and her brothers.

The fear of suicide wore everyone down as weeks slipped by. Miraculously, there was a favorable change in Rose's outlook. She began to accept her inevitable fate and realized how much she was hurting everyone who loved her most. This was certainly not her intention; she was remorseful and ashamed. For her own welfare and for the love of her family, Rose tried her best to go on with her life.

Because she was so familiar with the kitchen, Rose continued working alongside her mother. This was to be her personal refuge. Though, her sight was almost gone entirely, she possessed a natural dexterity, especially for all things culinary. Carolina was amazed at what her daughter could still do without sight. Eventually, Rose expressed desire to learn Braille; this would open up a new world for her. In the meantime, the radio became a vital part of her daily life. It was a great source of entertainment and joy. Her family members were jubilant to see Rose's transition to a more contented frame of mind. Something that had seemed impossible months earlier had been attained.

At this time, the family decided to get their own telephone in the house instead of continuing to go to a local store to make a call. In a few weeks, a phone was installed to the delight of Rose and her brothers. Most people did not have a phone in their house at that time, and only the wealthy had such a luxury item. With Giuseppe and the boys working, they were able to afford it. The convenience of the telephone and hearing the daily radio programs boosted Rose's spirits tremendously.

In a short time, with the help of others, she had transformed herself into a better and stronger person. This happened none too soon, for within a month, Rose lost the remainder of whatever vision she had left. It was apparent that the local pharmacist who first examined her eyes was correct in predicting that her vision would be gone within a year; it was exactly eleven months since that fateful day.

Jimmy

Jimmy was the oldest, and his role in the family was significant; his siblings, especially his brothers, looked up to him. He was the bridge between the old culture and the new and personified the image and expectations of what the oldest should be. The fact that he was two to twelve years older qualified him to be a disciplinarian and an advisor. With that said, he was loved, for he always had his siblings' best interest in mind. Jimmy was born in Italy and arrived in America as an infant. Thus, he was raised as an American and possessed knowledge of its history and culture. But the new ways were alien and intimidating to his old school parents. Giuseppe and Carolina relied on their first-born tremendously. With his help, they were able to handle and guide their young family in their new country.

If anyone asked Frank, Tony, Dominick, or Carl to describe their brother Jimmy, they would jokingly call him The Enforcer. He would intervene if he thought they were trying to pull the wool over their parents' eyes.

During his mid-teens, Jimmy went to work with his father to learn the shoe industry. Giuseppe was a master shoemaker and highly respected, so much so, that competing shoe firms were always offering better paying positions, but he chose to remain loyal to the company he worked for. After a number of years in this atmosphere, Jimmy also became a master shoemaker, but he didn't stop there. His innovative designs for new lines of shoes drew the attention of the company's executive management. They offered him a position as top designer in that installation, and his father couldn't have been more proud. Jimmy accepted the offer with enthusiasm and stayed at this position for a year and a half. Because the quality of his work was superb and his managerial skills had become obviously valued, he was approached once again by top management.

One morning, as Jimmy was at his drawing board, he was called away to a meeting with other executives who represented the company in other regions of the country. When he entered the boardroom, he felt a little intimidated by all the company brass. This soon passed, as each executive greeted him and introduced himself. Their exuberance was contagious, and Jimmy melded into this element easily. They all were respectful and gracious, and informed him that his performance was admirable and they had come to a decision. They offered Jimmy a chance to be trained as a regional director. He was happy and temporarily at a loss for words, but he responded affirmatively. Everyone present patted him on the back with their cheerful approval.

At supper that night, his parents and siblings celebrated Jimmy's promotion. Along with his future high-level position came a salary increase of one hundred percent. Such an increase would ensure the family economic stability never before dreamed of. In addition, because of his indomitable spirit, he would truly become even more of a role model to his younger brothers. But it was Dominick who Jimmy was grooming to be the first professional in the family.

When he came home from school, Dominick would approach Jimmy with questions about history and literature. Though Jimmy had never gone to college, he had always been a voracious reader. As a result of his older brother's guidance and insistence, Dominick excelled enough to enter a prodigious boys school. It was Jimmy who made sure his younger brother would study and do his homework. Dominick soon realized he was at an age which would soon define his future. Every day he would commute to school by trolley, leaving his neighborhood and friends behind. This was the most difficult of all to deal with. Deep down, he knew if he was going to amount to something, he would have to forego life as he knew it in his neighborhood. He would come home straight from school and hit the books. This would become his new routine. His academic standing in school demanded his full attention and effort. It was a tough transition when his old friends would come to call and he didn't have time to spend with them. It was challenging for Dominick to maintain good grades, but he did. Jimmy's encouragement and support were central factors in his dedication to succeed.

Meanwhile, Jimmy was evolving into a businessman. He would disappear in the early morning with his leather portfolio tucked under his arm and would not return sometimes twelve hours later. Many evenings his sister or Carolina would keep his food warm, for he usually arrived an hour or so after supper. Soon his work would take him on overnight trips to Boston and Utica, New York. The trips were to familiarize him with the operation of the plants. Many times Jimmy would receive accolades for his innovative design ideas and managerial prowess. Within six months, his reputation in the custom shoe industry was spreading throughout the northeast. Other competing companies began making tempting offers for him to join their ranks. Jimmy would never consider them, for like his father, he wanted to remain loyal to the company.

Nearly a year later, Jimmy's life was even more hectic. He gave all he had every day to the best of his ability. He vehemently refused to acknowledge the ill effects of the long hours. It was obvious that he was tiring and those around him noticed, especially Giuseppe. He saw his hardworking son's energy level being compromised. He seemed to lose vitality which had become his signature. When Jimmy was asked about it, he would pooh-pooh it and say he would try to get more rest. Still ignoring the advice, he continued to push himself by taking on new projects. He was initiating a new line of custom shoes that would be introduced in the fall. It was becoming a habit to come home, scarf down dinner, and disappear into his room and the solace of his drawing board. His overnight trips seemed to be more frequent as well, and his lethargy increased.

Finally, one night after supper, Giuseppe and Carolina beckoned Jimmy to remain at the table to talk. He listened to what they had to say and reluctantly agreed that he needed to slow down.

The following few weeks, to the relief of his parents, there was a definitely a decrease in his hectic schedule. Even with these changes, Jimmy's overall energy had not improved. His brothers were now aware of his inattentiveness which was out of character. They almost missed his critical, opinionated surveillance of their actions.

One morning Jimmy called out to his father from his bed. "Pop, I hate to do this to you, but could you tell them I won't be at work today? I'm not able, but I'll be alright if I just get some rest. Also tell them I will make up the work tomorrow."

"Are you okay? What's wrong?" Giuseppe asked with concern.

"Nah, nothing that won't pass. Just a bellyache."

"No worries, I will tell them, my son. They will certainly understand."

Giuseppe noticed Carolina's worried expression when he walked back into the kitchen. He tried to assure her that Jimmy just needed rest, but she could not be swayed from her fearful concern. Rose had just made her way to the kitchen and felt the melancholy mood in the air. "Pop, Momma, what is it?" she asked, knitting her brows.

"Your brother is too ill to work today," Giuseppe answered.

"That's not like him. He must be really sick to miss work," Rose commented, "He loves it so."

"We have to call Dr. Lorenzo and tell him to come," Carolina decided, "Let's not wait. Jimmy hasn't been himself for more than a month."

"Cara mia, you are right. This has been going on too long a time," Giuseppe agreed and then turned to hug her. "It will be alright once the doctor sees him." Carolina buried her head against her husband's chest and cried. She did not have a good feeling.

Later that morning, the doctor arrived. Dr. Lorenzo was also a longtime friend of the family, and he felt a sincere need to tell them not to be alarmed. He left the three in the kitchen to tend to Jimmy. He emerged again in twenty minutes and appeared pokerfaced. Dr. Lorenzo reiterated that they should not to worry unnecessarily and that Jimmy was quite run down and had probably eaten something that made him ill. The doctor believed the young man should have total rest and prescribed a blood-building tonic when he could tolerate it. Even though Jimmy's immunity seemed to be compromised, the doctor believed he would rebound within a week.

One positive result from Jimmy's convalescence was his reconnection with his sister and younger brothers. During this time, when he was not resting in bed and able to get out of bed despite the constant stomach pain, he would sit in the living room or the kitchen. His presence in the house dampened any back talk that might arise from his siblings to their parents. His brothers were glad to have him around. Dominick received his attention the most, for he was the one Jimmy felt exceptional affection for.

Two days went by, and Jimmy's condition was worsening. His family sadly witnessed his progressive physical decline and increasing pain. By the third day, he was totally bedridden. Everyone prayed for his recovery, but there was an underlining air of futility. The doctor now was visiting twice a day, but he offered little encouragement. The final diagnosis was peritonitis from an unknown cause, and there was no known medical procedure that would improve the situation.

Everyone took turns sitting beside Jimmy to keep him as comfortable as possible. He seemed to be aware of his dire condition and realized the inevitable was approaching. Nourishment was not possible, for not even a spoonful of broth could pass his lips. He was reduced to sip water through a straw with someone's help. Carolina and Giuseppe could barely refrain from breaking down when they were with him. Sensing their grief, Jimmy would weakly extend his finger to touch them, letting them know he would be alright. "Please bring Rose in," he whispered to his mother, and soon, his sister made her way to his bedside. She raised her hand until she touched his face. "Rose, you have a lot to deal with. With the help of Mom and Pop and your brothers, you will never be alone," he said weakly. "I am so very proud of you and what you are enduring." He paused to catch his breath and closed his eyes before continuing, "You have to promise me that you won't harm yourself again. It would destroy everyone in the family. Remember I will always love you."

"I love you, too, my dear brother."

"I'm getting too tired and need to rest a little." Jimmy closed his eyes, and Rose patted his cheek, looking at the face she loved the only way she could—with her fingertips. She withdrew her hand as he slipped into a sound sleep. Rose and her parents silently left the room.

The four boys gathered around the dining room table as the three sadly joined them. Carolina bravely managed to go to the kitchen to warm some leftovers for everyone.

They all picked at their food in silence. Afterward, Carolina and Rose went through the motions of putting things away. Tony decided to check on Jimmy and disappeared into his bedroom. It wasn't long until Tony emerged. He told them that Jimmy was awake and was requesting to see everyone. They looked at each other with an ominous look of anticipation and slowly filed into the small room. He motioned for them to come closer. His parents and Rose stood on one side, and his brothers on the other. They all leaned in to listen as he faintly said, "While I still can, I want to tell all of you how blessed I am for having all of you." He paused a while to gather his strength to continue. "Momma, Pop, what can I say? Thank you for your unwavering love. Rose, you are the best sister a brother could have. Remember you will never be alone as long as your brothers are around." He looked toward them, and slowly continued, "I want you guys...to promise me to take care...and look after your sister." They all nodded affirmatively in response.

"You have our word," promised Frank, "I will make sure of that." The others seconded his pledge. Jimmy nodded with a gentle smile.

"Dom," Jimmy said, motioning to Dominick to come closer. "Please, make me happy and try to stay in Boys High. Graduate. Go to college and become a lawyer. I know you can do it." Jimmy paused and swallowed, pain contorting his face for a few seconds before he added, "Do it for the family." Dominick hesitated.

"Jimmy, I'll do my best," Dominick responded. Jimmy settled back onto his pillow and whispered, "I love you all."

"We love you, Son," Giuseppe answered, choking on tears as Carolina pressed her cheek to his hand and sobbed.

"Let me sleep a while...I will see you again. I will be alright." Jimmy closed his eyes and was soon asleep. The sound of his labored breathing filled the room. They decided to have someone by his side at all times.

Carolina was the first to remain with him for a few hours. She grasped a string of worn rosary beads from her apron pocket and began to pray.

Jimmy was her firstborn. He was less than a year old when she brought him to America. She recalled the experience of the voyage on the ship with her brother at the turn of the century. She continued praying and fondly remembering Jimmy's life as a joyous, hopeful youth. Tears streamed down her cheeks as she pressed the beads between her fingers. In a while, Carolina involuntarily succumbed to sleep. Heartbroken and exhausted, she dreamed of happier days.

Giuseppe tossed and turned, and realized that Carolina was overdue in waking him for his turn in the vigil. Not surprised to find her asleep in the chair with the rosary on her lap, Giuseppe whispered, "Cara mia, go to bed. I will take over. Get some rest." Carolina stirred and gave in to retire for the night.

Giuseppe took his place by Jimmy's side. He, too, remembered his son growing up. He smiled. Jimmy had always been very bright and alert, and would do anything for his family. Giuseppe was filled with pride. He would never have dreamed that his son would go from helping him make shoes to designing them. Jimmy's positive, hopeful attitude was contagious and was loved by those around him.

In less than an hour, Giuseppe was also overcome by sleep and drifted into dreams. Hours passed before Tony entered the bedroom and found his father asleep in the chair. It pained him to see the suffering unfolding before him. He shook his head at the sad situation and gently removed his father's eyeglasses before they slipped off. Giuseppe woke, and Tony helped him toward the door.

Tony sat beside his ailing brother, and in the dim light of a lamp, buried his attention in a Western novel to momentarily escape the stark reality. Tony, tired from the emotional drain of the day and the sound of Jimmy's labored breathing, caught himself a number of times surrendering to an inviting slumber. To counter this, he got up and walked around the room. Tony returned to his Zane Grey novel when he thought he was alert enough. The hours passed slowly as he barely managed to fight off sleep until it was time to wake Frank, but before he could, Frank was already in the doorway.

Frank sat down by his failing brother and gently pulled the blanket up to Jimmy's chin. He touched Jimmy's forehead, and it seemed unusually cool. He also noticed that he didn't see or hear his brother breathing. With a sinking feeling in his stomach, Frank lifted Jimmy's hand to get a pulse. He couldn't detect one. He tried the other hand, but it was the same result. He knew he must wake his father.

Frank went to their parents' room and put his hand gently on Giuseppe's shoulder. "Pop, wake up. It's Jimmy." His father shook his head and slowly came out of a restless sleep. Frank told him once again. Giuseppe was motionless until the impact of the reality set in. He told Frank to go to the hallway and phone the doctor to come.

In the meantime, Dominick was awake and heading toward the kitchen. He heard crying coming from Jimmy's room. He entered and saw his father crying and hugging his limp, silent brother. Dominick's worst nightmare was unfolding. The fifteen year old, with tears streaking his cheeks, went to console his grieving father.

Frank came rushing back and said the doctor would arrive as soon as possible. Carolina, who had been sleeping, was awakened by the hurried footsteps and commotion in Jimmy's room. Shaking off her fatigue, she worriedly went to her son's room. When she saw

Giuseppe hugging Jimmy, her worst fears had come true. She began wailing uncontrollably. Frank embraced their inconsolable mother while Tony went to get Rose. Carolina managed to say, "Figlio mio, please don't leave, not yet."

Rose, who had already heard the sobbing, felt her way to Jimmy's room. Once there, she asked, "Jimmy passed, didn't he?"

"Yes, Rose, it looks like it," Frank said with a nod.

"I had a dream that he was telling me he was going to be fine and not to worry about him." Rose started to cry and went to her grief-stricken parents. They all held each other and sobbed.

The doctor finally arrived as Dominick led him to Jimmy's room. When he entered, everyone instantly made room for him to get closer. He hurriedly put his stethoscope to Jimmy's chest for the slightest sign of a heartbeat. In the anxious moments following his examination, he shook his head in sad defeat. "He passed in his sleep about an hour ago or so," Dr. Lorenzo concluded.

With the loss of Jimmy, a bright light of hope was forever extinguished. The absence of his energy would scar those left behind for decades to come.

Jimmy's death shattered Dominick's drive and ambition. He seemed to have lost his purpose and any future goal. Immediately, his grades began to plummet at Boys' High. It had been Jimmy who encouraged and monitored Dominick's progress, and without him, incentive was lost. The neighborhood and the streets were once again tempting distractions for the grieving fifteen year old. It was a difficult struggle. In the past, he could always count on Jimmy to be there to talk to and help him with his studies. Giuseppe was too busy trying to make a living and was not always available. The real impediment was Giuseppe's inability to fully comprehend the English language as well as the American culture. He, of course, attempted to help his son, but it was too perplexing. Giuseppe felt frustrated and helpless, and the academic responsibility was to rest solely on Dominick's shoulders. He tried his best to cope with schoolwork but lacked the initiative he once had. It wasn't long until he dropped out of school and resigned himself to an uncertain future.

Goose Showed 'em

Of all the guys in the neighborhood, Goose by far was the best runner. His long, lanky legs could eat up a lot of distance real fast. In school he was always picked for the long relay races. For the most part, he was jovial and quick to join in.

Goose was brought up by his widower father, for his mother had passed away when he was only five years old. He and his older sister worked after school to help their father get by. As a freshman in high school, the athletic coach tried to in vain to get him to join the track team. He turned it down, for he thought it would interfere with his much-needed part time job as a delivery boy. Not being on the track team did not deter him from his passion for running on his own terms.

In the neighborhood, there were a few young, bold men who wanted to become boxers. Goose, though much younger, would accompany them on their runs during their workouts. He did it to stay in shape and had a secret dream to someday compete in the Olympics. In the meantime, he participated in long distance events. It was not uncommon to see him running early in the morning and would jog for miles without showing any sign of fatigue. He finally realized he could work this to his advantage.

He began to spread the word to as many people as possible that if they needed to get an urgent message delivered in most parts of Brooklyn, he could do it. Many professionals who did not trust the postal system to promptly deliver important documents called on him. To the surprise of many in the neighborhood, it turned out that Goose was faster on foot than some of the expensive couriers of the time. Goose was even teased about this fact, but it didn't faze him much, for he was making money to help his father and sister.

In September, there was an annual five mile race that wound its way through the streets of Brooklyn and was open to all runners. The route would begin and end at the intersection of Empire and Washington; participants would run east on Empire then make a left on Troy and head north to Atlantic Ave. From here they would run east on Atlantic to Washington Ave., turning south. This was the last leg of the race to the finish line on Empire.

Despite neighborhood cynics, all of Goose's friends wanted him to enter the race and believed he would have an excellent chance of winning. After they urged him to do it, he finally signed up half-heartedly. Some of the entrants were seasoned runners while others were high school and college track stand-outs. Regardless, anyone was welcome to participate.

As word got around that he entered the race, the local bookies were already giving odds. The days prior to the event, Goose began to feel the pressure of his pending performance. He did not want to let his friends down. Goose realized that some of the entrants were more experienced runners, and he had serious doubts about his capability.

The day of the race was an extremely foggy Sunday. Regardless, the event would still be held. Goose, accompanied by twenty or so of his friends and supporters, took the trolley to Empire Blvd. which was the starting place and finish line. Goose was issued number sixteen to pin on the front and back of his shirt. His friends joked that his number reflected his age, which they thought was a portent of good luck.

All the runners soon lined up to the mark. There were forty impatient participants waiting for the blast of the starting pistol. Then the anticipated shot resounded, and they all took off running east on Empire. Since it would be a long race, there wasn't much vying for position. All of Goose's friends made themselves as comfortable as possible, finding places to sit on the sidewalk and along the curb. Other spectators did likewise as they settled near the finish line. In less than thirty minutes the race would be over.

The big wagers who bet on the race had a way to keep informed of the runners' progress. One such individual was Shady Augie who had his associate in a phone booth near Troy and St. Mark's. His friend was to call him when the runners came by and report where number sixteen was located in the pack. Augie, after some waiting and monopolizing the phone booth, got the call that number sixteen was in eighth place. Further along the route, Augie's Uncle Johnny lived on Atlantic Ave. near Washington Ave., and from there, would report on Goose's position. Soon Uncle Johnny called and reported that number sixteen was fourth. Excited Augie couldn't wait to tell the others about Goose's progress. When the others heard, they were hopeful for a good finish.

It was the last leg of the race as the runners came down Washington Ave. south to Empire Blvd. They ran toward the anxious spectators near the finish line. The weather was still foggy, and it was difficult to see further than a quarter of a mile. Bach, who was in the crowd, had brought his father's World War I binoculars. He focused north but couldn't make out much because of the poor visibility. Finally, out of the mist, he spotted a lone runner approaching. The rest of the pack wasn't in sight. "This guy is way ahead of the rest, but I don't think it's Goose," Bach told Dominick and Red. "I don't know who this guy is, but he must be a block ahead of everyone else." Bach continued to focus on the sole runner then suddenly yelled out, "I don't believe this! I think it's Goose! Holy crap, it is! It's number sixteen!" Everyone from the neighborhood went wild. Their awkward sixteen-year-old friend had outdistanced veteran runners. Within moments, Goose clearly came into view with a big grin and crossed the finish line seconds later. His friends rushed over to him and victoriously hoisted him up onto their shoulders as he shook his head in disbelief.

For days afterward, the neighborhood glowed with pride for their modest, young champion.

Cold, Hard Times

It was almost eight years after Jimmy's death and the third year of the Depression, and economic conditions were still dire for most. Just having a roof over one's head and getting enough to eat was paramount.

Dominick—now in his twenties—was unemployed like the majority, and spending his idle days in the aisles of the Brooklyn Library. He had come to value and look forward to time spent with his head buried in books. In a way, he felt he was redeeming himself with his rededication to learning. He was suffering from guilt for breaking his promise to Jimmy and for dropping out of high school years before.

During the last days of November, extremely cold weather took hold in the Northeast; snowstorms came twice a week. The outlook for Christmas and the new year was dismal. The lack of money put a grim shroud of futility over the suffering majority. It seemed that the only people who were employed worked for the government, the state, or the city. Private positions such as small business in the building trades were almost non-existent. Families were forced to auction off and sell anything of value which was usually sold to pay for basic necessities. It was a common sight to see dejected people waiting on long soup lines. Something was drastically wrong and unfair. The "geniuses" in business and government were absolutely inept in fixing it. The excessive misappropriation of funds and indifference inflicted incalculable hardship on the general public. The repeal of Prohibition, lasting for over a decade, seemed to be the only bone cast to a drowning economy.

The holidays came and went with a solemn tone, and most people were glad to see them over with. From the beginning of January, snow had come more frequently, and the idle jobless could only stare out their frost-covered windows and dream. The depth of the snow was mounting in the streets and became too large an undertaking to clear all the miles of roads. Only the major thoroughfares were maintained by the city plows. As a result, the borough was forced to hire any able-bodied person who could wield a snow shovel. They were offering four dollars a day to men who hadn't worked in many months. For them, this was a great opportunity. Dominick and his brother Carl, and now married brother Frank, enlisted in the snow shovel brigade.

Dominick trudged through knee-deep snow along Schenectady Ave. in a quest for work. An empty store had been taken over by the city to hire men who were willing to shovel snow. When he arrived, Dominick waited in line for his turn to be hired. He was surprised to see old friends he hadn't seen in years—among them was Red, still rusty-haired and affable. They managed to make a good time of it despite the desperation of all. It felt like a school reunion as he also reacquainted himself with forgotten friends.

Dominick flipped up the collar of his long winter coat to protect his ears from the harsh wind as he patiently walted. It was a sharp, cold day, and everyone had their hands buried deep in their pockets for warmth. Their white, frosty breath engulfed their faces while some stomped their feet to get the blood going.

In line behind Dominick was a young man named Jasper who had the aura of a newly arrived immigrant. During their conversation, the man spoke with an obvious Italian accent. Dominick was surprised to hear that he was from a town in Calabria, not far from where his parents Giuseppe and Carolina had lived. The common ground didn't stop there. This man's father was also a shoemaker.

Dominick and his new friend from Italy were issued push snow shovels and then instructed to go to the middle of the block and join the other men. When they arrived, the foreman of the crew told them to push the snow into the sewers which had their heavy covers removed. If the snow was too far from the openings, the men were to make piles near the curb which would be removed later. The main objective was to open the street for travel.

It was close to seven o'clock that evening when Dominick was informed to stop shoveling. It was none too soon, for he was tired. He slowly walked toward home, and the stars flickered brightly as the long day finally came to an end. Muscles hurt that he didn't know he had. It had been some time since he had done that kind of physical labor.

Dinner was on the table when he half-stumbled in. He barely ate and kept nodding off. Dominick finally surrendered and flopped into bed. He slept soundly until eight o'clock the next morning.

Dominick and his new friend Jasper decided they would rather work the night shift from twelve a.m. to eight a.m. because it paid six dollars instead of four. The two young men met up at the storefront office and picked up their shovels. This time a truck drove them a few blocks away to work on other snow-covered streets.

Dominick asked Jasper if he could call him Jay. Jasper agreed and liked the sound of it because it sounded more American. Along with others, the two friends worked and cleared more that night than what was expected of them. Time passed, and they finished early. About six o'clock a.m., with their shovels in their hands, Dominick and Jay walked a block over to Bergen St. to visit Jay's Uncle Bruno. There, Bruno had a small leather shop and was a very early riser. So when they knocked on his door, he was already awake and drinking coffee. When he saw his nephew and his friend, he happily welcomed them in. With the temperature hovering about ten degrees, Jay and Dominick were grateful to get out of the cold. Bruno offered them hot coffee and a shot of Italian anisette which they readily accepted. Bruno wasn't married, and lived and worked in his small shop. Dominick was impressed with the fine leather belts, handbags, and gloves Jay's uncle had crafted.

The two young men stayed and talked to the older man about the old days in the small town in Calabria where he was raised. Because of Bruno's hospitality and good conversation, the time slipped by unnoticed. It was quarter after seven before they realized it, and the two visitors had to leave for the walk back to where they would be picked up at quarter to eight for their ride home. Jay and Dominick said their goodbyes and thanked the man for his hospitality. Bruno told them they could visit any time they were near his shop.

They returned to the street which was totally cleared of snow and waited to be picked up by the foreman. He was on time and drove the friends back to the storefront where they dropped off their shovels.

A little after eight a.m., Dominick opened the door to the kitchen where his family had just finished eating breakfast. He was glad to hand his mother the six dollars he earned that night. He was unaware that his brother Carl had also worked the day shift shoveling snow and had brought home four dollars. Within twenty-four hours, the family had a windfall of ten dollars which would really help to buy necessities.

Both sons continued to remove snow during that winter and considered themselves fortunate to be able to help their needy family.

Times were bad, and to lighten their spirits, the local men would gather discarded wood from vacant lots and pile it high to light bonfires. They would also roast potatoes, play instruments, and sing songs. The warmth and the light from a blazing fire was comforting. Most did the best they could with what was dealt to them.

By this time, Dominick's older brothers had already married. Frank and his new wife were only a few blocks away, and Tony and his bride moved to a small town in Jersey. Giuseppe would work a day or so a week when the shoe factory had orders to fill, which was sporadic. Dominick and Carl were the two income producers if there was work to be had.

The only reliable businesses were the small local food stores and the bars that reopened after Prohibition ended. The vacant stores where businesses once thrived reflected the times. This personified the mood during this harsh period. People shuffled along city streets with sullen faces and hopeless expressions.

One of the brighter distractions was the entertainment field, in particular, the movies. They were a great antidote and tranquilizer. For a few pennies, one could lose himself amid scores of joyful musicals. People exited the theaters with happier outlooks even if it was temporary. The other relatively new phenomenon was radio. Unlike the movies, one did not have to leave the house to enjoy it and was in almost every home. It was available to the most remote sections of America where towns were many miles apart. The magic of turning the dial and hearing Al Jolson, Eddie Cantor, Will Rogers, Burns and Allen, Fibber McGee and Molly, Amos and Andy, Bing Crosby, Kate Smith, and Jack Benny was an immediate pleasure. It was a godsend to the poor, shut-ins, and those who lived in isolated parts of the country. No other single form of entertainment or communication came close to radio's positive influence on such a large scale and definitely eased some of the despair and pain of an entirely failed system.

To everyone's joy, the cold months of winter finally came to an end. Though Dominick still spent the majority of his time with his head always in books, he finally had an opportunity for a real job with one of the largest painting contractors on Long Island.

The lead came through Giuseppe who was good friends with a successful member of the Sons of Italy society to which he belonged. This respected man owned the company and was known by all by Amadeo. He had come to America and built a thriving business during the 20s painting some of the wealthiest homes on Long Island. At this particular time, he was looking for someone new who he could train for the business. Luckily for Dominick, it fell right into his lap at a time when jobs were non-existent. One of the benefits was the fact that Amadeo lived only four blocks away and would pick up his workers who lived close by. So Dominick would be picked up every morning and brought back home at night.

When his first morning of work arrived, he waited on the front steps and hoped to make a good impression on his new boss. When Amadeo pulled up, there were three other workmen in the vehicle. Amadeo was a short man with a large mustache and a jovial expression. He quickly introduced himself and told Dominick how much he respected his father Giuseppe.

Dominick got in and they drove a few more blocks to pick up another worker. They took the most direct road out of Brooklyn toward Long Island. After driving thirty-five minutes, Amadeo pulled up to a stately mansion with an expansive manicured lawn. Everyone piled out, and the seasoned workers disappeared into the house as Amadeo pulled Dominick aside. He told him to stay close and just be an observer for now.

The amiable man met the woman of the house to discuss the colors she desired. She clutched swatches of cloth in her hand and informed Amadeo of which ones she had selected. With a handful of colored paint tubes, he began to mix them into a five gallon bucket of white. As he added the dabs of color, the paint came alive with the desired shade. In a short time, Amadeo had mixed the exact color to match the woman's fabric and repeated the process to produce the colors of the other swatches. Dominick was amazed at Amadeo's ability to get the exact shade of desired color.

His talent didn't end there. He was able to take a blank plaster wall and imitate a wood finish with knot holes and all. If the customer wanted a mural, Amadeo was talented enough to paint anything that was requested freehand. He was truly a master painter and was always in demand by rich home owners who would never settle for less than the best. There was a segment of society that, regardless of the economy, could perpetually afford the finest quality no matter what the cost.

Dominick continued to work for Amadeo for the next two years and enjoyed being part of a creative project. He was also grateful for his employer's graciousness and patience. Dominick was privy to high society culture and personalities he never thought existed.

Unfortunately, the position was not to last forever and came to an end one day when Amadeo called Dominick aside. He informed him that he must let him go, though to no fault in his performance. Business had deteriorated so much that Amadeo was forced to regretfully let a few men go. Amadeo was able to only keep a few painters who had been with him the longest. Dominick was at a loss but understood the circumstances.

When he was dropped off in front of his house for the last time, Dominick sadly waved farewell to his good-natured mentor and watched him drive away. Within a week, Dominick retreated back into his sanctuary at the library. As millions of others, he was idle once again. He was used to the old routine of getting up and walking the dismal streets to the library where he would remain for most of the day before returning home. Books about ancient cultures and the Renaissance were his only escape from the drudgery of everyday survival. It was also a good distraction from his hungry belly and gave him a reasonable excuse to not go home to eat; Dominick figured there would be more food to go around for his parents, Carl, or Rose. And his new habit of cigarette smoking conveniently took the edge off his appetite.

Dominick was also seeing more of his friend Jay who now was working at a machine shop next to the Brooklyn Bridge. This was very timely because Dominick received a tip that a small machine shop was looking for help. When he told Jay about the job, Jay expressed in helping him. He showed Dominick how to use micrometer and calipers that were used in manufacturing parts.

The next day Dominick took the subway to the heavy industrial area of Brooklyn where the shop was located. The foreman who would be his boss took him on a tour of the floor where he would be working. Dominick's first impression was that of a Dickens novel—the loud overhead belts screeched above the heads of the stress-weary workers. He and the foreman walked by, and by doing so, seemed to add to the tension already there. In less than twenty minutes, the interview was concluded. Dominick was glad to leave and head back home.

A few days later, without any word about the job, he was not that disappointed in the fact that he hadn't heard anything. By the end of the week, he finally got a phone call. The job was his if he wanted it. So, with little enthusiasm but little choice, Dominick accepted the offer. Because of Jay's quick, concise instruction in machinery he would start on Monday the following week.

He begrudgingly began his new job, arriving punctually. He was politely shown his work area and introduced to the other men. The worker next to him was assigned to instruct and help him learn the use of milling machines, lathes, and drill presses.

The first week passed without incident as Dominick absorbed the rudiments involved in the work. But to his surprise, he took to this new vocation effortlessly, for he liked the exactness of the work. After three weeks, Dominick was producing the same amount of pieces as those who had been there for years. A month passed slowly, but Dominick didn't mind too much because he was helping his family. A lot of inequities were overlooked because of the sake of necessity.

Ralph, the foreman, became increasingly cruel to everyone. He was never a compassionate person, but by all accounts, he was becoming intolerable. His attitude was such that everyone despised the mere sight of him. Whenever he approached the machine operators, he would drop the metal plates on the floor and then shove them with his foot toward his employees. Most cursed him under their breath, but no one said anything for fear of losing their jobs. Some would just cower and almost shake in fear of any retaliation. It was obvious that Ralph realized he could easily intimidate people and used this to his full advantage. For some reason, when he brought Dominick's work to him, he restrained from using intimidation. Instead, Ralph would put the work on the floor and say, "When you get the time, please work on this."

There was also Hank, another worker who was not a target of this bullying. He and Dominick had discussed how to help the older, desperate workers who took the brunt of his insane outbursts. More resentment built up each day that went by. Dominick informed Hank that he did not know how much longer he could go on witnessing the ever increasing abuse and injustice.

One day Ralph's aggressiveness had reached a new level of cruelty. As usual, he handed out the work to be done by throwing it on the floor and demanding that the workers pick it up immediately. He then ordered them to thank him for the work. No one responded to this new level of disrespect; most kept their heads bowed and said, "thank you." Dominick watched each cowering worker obey the tyrant.

The bullying foreman worked his way down the line toward Dominick who was already seething. When Ralph reached Dominick's station, he placed the work on the floor and said, "You, I won't ask to say 'thank you.'" Dominick bent over and lifted the work onto his bench table. The foreman was about to walk away when Dominick called to him.

"Ralph, I've got something for you," Dominick said calmly. The puzzled, obnoxious man came over and put his face close. Dominick then pushed his work off the table back onto the floor. Just as Ralph's eyes traveled from the floor and back up at Dominick, he was stunned by a right upper cut to the chin. The impact of Dominick's punch lifted Ralph over a bench behind him and went head over heels to the other side. He was out cold.

The onlookers were in total disbelief. Most agreed he had it coming for a long time, but no one had the nerve to do it. Hank rushed over to Dominick's side and suggested, "Dom, gather your things and leave before someone calls the cops and he wakes up. Just go."

Dominick took his advice and exited the building in a hurry and headed toward home. When he arrived, Rose and their mother were surprised to see him so early. He told them the job wasn't working out, and he decided to quit. It wasn't like Dominick to quit a job, but they figured he must have had a good reason to do so.

That evening, Dominick expected the worst every time the phone rang. Not wanting to worry his family, he did not say anything more about what had taken place. Finally, later that night, Carolina pulled him aside and asked him what was bothering him. Dominick confessed to her what happened and told her not to tell the rest of the family, which she agreed to.

He left the house the next day before noon and told everyone he'd be at the library. When he arrived, he took a seat near the front entrance and made himself comfortable reading a James Fennimore Cooper novel. Dominick's attention was distracted numerous times, for every time someone entered, he thought it was someone coming to arrest him.

He stayed for the remainder of the day and finally left at five-thirty to go home. When he opened the door to the kitchen, he glanced at his mother, who shook her head with a half-smile, letting him know that everything was alright. With a sigh of relief, Dominick sat down and ate with the others.

He went by unscathed that night, as well as the next day, and the day after that. A week passed and still no repercussions. Dominick began to feel more at ease. The second and third week elapsed without consequence. He then completely forgot about the incident until a month later. While walking along the street, Dominick met his friend Hank. He informed Dominick that he also was not working at the machine shop. He had quit a few weeks after Dominick. Hank went on to tell his friend that things changed after Ralph was knocked out cold. When the abusive foreman returned to work after recovering for a few weeks from a broken jaw, he was a different man. Ralph readjusted his attitude as people began to step forward and tell him how cruel and intimidating he had been to everyone. His change in character was a welcome relief. Hank continued, "I heard from others that now when Ralph approaches the men with their work, he places it on their work table and asks them politely to do the job." Dominick was surprised.

"I can't believe it. Are you sure it's the same guy?" Dominick asked, shaking his head and smiling.

"Apparently, the jerk had an epiphany and changed his ways entirely. The men told me to tell you 'thanks'. They aren't stressed about going to work anymore."

After the chance meeting with his friend, Dominick couldn't believe that good came from a physical altercation and walked away relieved, free from guilt and feeling better about himself.

The Shakedown

It was a windy winter day as the sun meekly made an appearance. Dominick walked briskly toward home after being gone a few hours that Saturday morning. He bought the *Brooklyn Eagle* at the newsstand and then walked the next few blocks home. To avoid the icy wind, he tucked his scarf closer to his neck and pulled his cap down further to keep it from flying off.

Once in the warmth of the hallway, he unbuttoned his coat. He heard loud opera music coming from the other side of door as he reached to open it. It seemed a little odd, for his father usually played his opera records at night after supper. He shrugged and went in.

Once in the kitchen, he saw his mother standing with a very serious expression. She looked toward Dominick and put a finger to her lips for him to be quiet. He glanced toward the dining room and saw his father talking to a seedy-looking stranger who was standing with his right hand in his coat pocket. Instantly concerned, Dominick asked, "What's goin' on, Pop? Who's this guy?"

"It's okay, my son. I have this under control. There has been a misunderstanding," Giuseppe said, cautiously. Dominick then looked to his right and saw his sister Rose seated in a chair in an anxious state and a sleazy-looking woman on the other side of her. Next to her was Carl, and judging from his expression, he was fuming. Giuseppe attempted to reassure his son, "Carlo, basta, calm down. Don't make the situation worse than what it is."

"Pop, will you please tell me what the hell is going on?" Dominick addressed his father once again, this time with little patience. Before Giuseppe could answer, Carl yelled out.

"Dom, these bastards are trying to shake us down!" Hearing this, Dominick instinctively took a step toward the man who then reacted by pulling out a revolver.

"Mister, you better move back unless you wanna get shot," ordered the intruder.

"Calm down. No one will get hurt. My son, I told you, I will handle this," Giuseppe pleaded with his son. "This man is under the ridiculous impression that we have thousands of dollars in the house."

"Well, you and your girlfriend are both nuts," Dominick said to the guy, "I don't know where you got your information. Like everyone else, we're barely making it. I don't know what imbecile told you we had money."

"That's not what I heard. We got it from a good source

that you guys are loaded," said the shifty thug.

"Buddy, you're insane, and the person who told you this lie is even crazier!" Dominick responded with anger.

Just then, Frank came in the house, and like Dominick, instantly sized up the situation. "Who the hell are you two? If this is what I think it is, you're wasting your time," Frank declared, already on the defense.

"We'll see about that," the man said, waving his pistol. "I wanna use the phone," he added, to which Giuseppe nodded. The female accomplice went to the phone and dialed a number. Apparently, she began to question their informant. Whoever she was speaking to was insistent that the money was in the house. The accomplice then hung up the phone and whispered something to her cohort. They both nodded in agreement. "Look," the man said, "we're going to search this place to see for ourselves."

Frank, who was streetwise, looked at his two brothers and insisted, "Dominick, Carl, I don't want you guys to do anything." Meanwhile, Giuseppe put his arms around Carl to quell his agitation and reminded him not to do anything stupid. The man with the revolver kept the situation in check as the woman went from closet to closet. She dumped out contents from drawers in every room, scattering the family's precious few possessions in every direction.

In the other room, Carl was infuriated and punched the wall. Giuseppe and Frank attempted to pacify raging Carl. Dominick stood close by the armed thug and waited for an opportunity to act. He remained cautious, for his sister was only arm's length away from the thief. The anxious intruder made it a point to keep his distance and not to get too close to any of the brothers.

Frank leaned toward his father and whispered, "Pop, don't worry. No one's going to get hurt. Our main concern right now is Carl. He's a powderkeg ready to explode. If Rose wasn't here, this would've been over by now. This Bonnie and Clyde would go out in an ambulance." Giuseppe wiped his forehead as he listened.

"No violence, my son. Be calm. When they see that we have no money, they will leave," Giuseppe insisted.

The woman walked back into the room shaking her head and looking at her accomplice. He grimaced at this revelation and glanced at Giuseppe. "We have to use the phone again," he boldly said. Giuseppe threw his hands up in frustration and nodded to keep the peace. The brazen thug dialed and then ranted to the person on the line who had given them faulty information. Everyone could hear that it was a woman's voice responding. The hood lambasted her with profanity and finally slammed down the phone. He then audaciously apologized to Giuseppe and the rest of the family for their actions. Stunned faces stared back at him. "I'm going to really make that bitch pay," he informed them as he and his female companion backed out of the house with his gun still drawn. They quickly descended the stairs and went out to the street. They looked over their shoulders and walked away as fast as they could.

Meanwhile, everyone in the family upstairs breathed easy and looked at each other in amazement at what had just taken place. Dominick was the first to remark, "Frank, you know these crackpots could come back again. We have to do something."

"Dom, don't worry," assured Frank. "I know someone who could take care of this problem."

"I hope so," Dominick said, "I'm afraid Momma, Pop, and Rose will be here alone if they come back."

"Look," interjected Carl, "at least one of us has to be home. We have to be ready for these bastards if they come back. I think we should get a gun for protection."

"Don't worry, Carl. I've got this covered," Frank insisted and then instantly acted.

He phoned his friend Mike and told him what had happened. Mike asked for a description of the would-be thieves, including clothing they were wearing and informed him he would call back Frank when he had some news.

Frank told everyone he would stay put until he received the crucial phone call. The family began to clean up the mess left by the intruders and cursed them and their ancestors while doing so.

The hours passed slowly and weighed heavily on everyone. Carolina, along with Rose, returned to the kitchen to prepare for supper. Within the hour they were all seated around the table as they had done hundreds of times before sharing a meal. After dinner and the table was cleared, Giuseppe got up to light his pipe and went to the window. He parted the curtain and looked down at the street. It was already dark and snowing lightly. As he stared out, he thought of his younger days in Italy and his small hometown in Calabria where times were simpler and happier. His family did not have many material things, for it wasn't costly to be happy. He almost regretted the decision he made fifty years earlier to come to America. The snow intensified, and his reverie continued. This was another component to his melancholy; Calabrian winters were mild and it only snowed in the mountains. He shook the memories aside and took another puff on his pipe.

Dominick sat at the end of the table reading a novel, and Frank was positioned by the phone reading the newspaper. Carl sat in an easy chair with his attention buried in a Western novel. Time dragged for all. Giuseppe distracted himself by reading an Italian newspaper. In the kitchen, Rose and Carolina listened to their favorite radio programs.

Two hours later, Dominick looked up from his book. It was twenty after eleven. Carl had already put his reading aside and had gone to the bedroom. Carolina and Rose were nodding off at the kitchen table until they finally gave into their drowsiness and went to bed. Giuseppe had fallen asleep in the sofa chair.

Dominick stayed up another fifteen minutes and then told Frank he'd be going to sleep but made his brother promise to wake him when Mike's call came through. "I promise I'll let you know when we get the call," Frank assured him.

Frank slumped back into his chair to wait out the vigil. Giuseppe was still asleep in the chair, despite the insistence of his family to go to bed. Time went by at a snail's pace until two hours later the silence was broken by the sharp ringing of the phone. Frank was jolted from his sleep and grabbed the phone. He heard Mike's forceful voice on the other end, "Frank, I took care of the problem. Don't worry. They're not going to bother your family anymore."

"Thanks a lot, Mike," Frank responded gratefully. "Who were they and what happened?"

"Two smalltime shakedown artists. This guy and his lady friend, I heard, were doing this to a lot of people. People were too scared to say anything for fear of getting beat up. Apparently, they heard about your family through a neighborhood woman who thought you guys had money." Mike paused. "By the way, after they left your house, they found the woman informant and beat her pretty good for the bad tip."

"I see," Frank said, listening.

"It didn't take that long to find this Bonnie and Clyde. These two dopes were very mouthy and that made it easier to find 'em."

"Where were they?"

"My associates found 'em few blocks away and worked them over and told them to get to hell outta the area, and that if they ever came back, they wouldn't live to see the next day. So Frank, tell the rest not to worry anymore."

"Mike, I don't know how to thank you," Frank said with gratitude. By the time he put the phone down, Giuseppe was awake and anxious to hear what had happened. Dominick and Carl were also awake and waiting in the doorway to hear about the fate of the two shysters.

Everyone was relieved that this time, all ended well.

Poker and Pool

During the 1920s and 30s, poolrooms occupied every section of Brooklyn. They were frequented by the average Joe, tradesmen, and businessmen. They all had one simple, common bond: they wanted to shoot pool. As always within any group, unsavory sorts existed, and they would look for easy pigeons upon which to prey. For the most part, these establishments attracted men who had some place to go after work. Such a place was Danny's, near the corner of Schenectady and Bergen. It was the ideal hangout to play cards, place a bet on a horse, or play the numbers. Because of its not-so-pristine reputation, the police would periodically raid the place. Most of the law's attempts were futile, but they still had a persistent desire to apprehend anyone involved in illegal activity, no matter how trivial.

One night Dominick and Frank met a mutual friend at Danny's. They were seated at a table and drinking coffee when the police burst in. The cops ordered everyone to line up against the wall. Frank leaned over and said, "I'm tellin' you, don't move. Act like nothing is wrong." Dominick looked at his brother as if he were crazy but thought he had nothing to lose. Frank and Dominick remained seated as the other patrons lined up against the far wall. A sergeant in charge approached the two and asked, "What's with you guys?"

"We've done nothin' wrong," Frank said calmly, "We just stopped in for a cup of coffee." The sergeant remained quiet for a second and looked at them.

"Okay, I'll buy that. Stay seated." Dominick almost fell out of his chair with surprise.

"Frank, how the hell did you know he was going to leave us alone?" Dominick asked when the cop walked away.

"That's easy," Frank answered, "Just act normal. You're not guilty. It works every time."

Everyone in the pool hall including Danny was marched outside to three police wagons. On the way out, Danny threw the keys to the place to Frank and told him to lock up when he and Dominick left. Once again, Dominick looked at his older brother in amazement. "If I wasn't here to witness it, I would never have believed it," confessed Dominick with a smile.

A month later, Danny came up with the brilliant idea of holding a poker tournament to drum up business. The news spread like wildfire, and all the locals and those outside the neighborhood showed a burning interest in the event. Because of such fervor, the match was scheduled to take place within a few days of the hush-hush announcement.

Things were rearranged inside the poolroom to accommodate ten tables. There would be five players to each table. To avoid any trouble with the law, no money would be permitted on the table and poker chips would be used instead. The chips were to be bought from the banker—in this case, Danny—and would be cashed in at the end of the night. There was an entry fee of twenty dollars to get into the match. This amount of money during those these times was a considerable amount, and it attracted only the most serious gamblers.

To Danny's surprise, fifty players signed up. Everyone in the neighborhood had a personal interest in it, for someone's father, brother, or friend would be playing. It was important not to arouse too much attention so the game would go unnoticed by the cops. Each entrant was required to buy a minimum of fifty dollars' worth of poker chips. The two players at each of the ten tables with the most chips at the end of the night would be eligible to go on to the next match. By the second night, there were twenty players remaining of the fifty, five at four tables. By the third night, eight remaining players played at two tables of four. When the last night arrived, there were four participants left in the final game.

Danny's place was jammed with spectators. The onlookers bet among themselves on which one of the four would be the ultimate winner. The bets were substantial, as odds were mounting. They were packed shoulder to shoulder, and to minimize prying eyes, police, and undesirables, the doors were locked and the shades were drawn.

The four remaining anxious players were the center of everyone's attention. That night only two kinds of poker were allowed—Five Card Draw and Five Card Stud. The four men were shrewd and experienced players and knew the odds of drawing certain hands and made their bets accordingly. The surviving finalists were at a table in the center of the room surrounded by most of the adult population from the neighborhood.

By the end of the first hour, one player was forced to withdraw from the competition when he ran out of chips. The three remaining men went on to play another hour and a quarter, until a second player was forced to quit. The two players left had stacks of red and blue chips piled in front of them. One of the finalists was a popular businessman from Bergen St. The other was a well-known, hardworking plumber from the neighborhood. Between them were thousands of dollars' worth of poker chips in the pot. They continued playing as the winning went back and forth between them. In time, they were almost equal in the amount of chips they each had won. It was one in the morning when the businessman suggested a challenge. He suggested one game of Five Card Stud, winner take all. His opponent looked at him and nodded, "Sure, why not?" It was a true gambler's dream. The room erupted with applause at the brave, high stakes challenge. Each player then shoved all of his winnings to the middle of the table.

Danny, the owner, ripped off the seal of a new deck and proceeded to shuffle the cards thoroughly and then had one of the players cut the deck. Danny would deal in this important final game. He dealt the first card face down to each and followed with the second card face-up. A king of hearts to the businessman and a jack of spades to the tradesman. The third card up was a ten of clubs to the businessman while a nine of diamonds was thrown to his opponent. Danny hesitated and then dealt the fourth card. Ten of hearts to the businessman and a seven of spades to the plumber. Danny waited a second and then threw the fifth card, a deuce of diamonds to the businessman and a queen of clubs to his opponent. This was the last card to be dealt.

The only thing showing was a pair of tens for the businessman while his opponent only had a queen high nothing. Danny said, "Gents, this is the moment of truth. Okay, turn your first card up." The businessman was the first to turn his card over to reveal a four of hearts, but he still had a pair of tens which looked good. The plumber smiled as he turned his card up. It was a queen of hearts. He had two queens, and with this, he threw his hands up in victory as all the bystanders clapped. It was a great competition.

Three weeks after the success of the poker match, the ever-enterprising Danny got another idea to make money. He had read and heard about Willie Mosconi, a young Italian-American pool player who was touted as an up and coming phenomenon. He had been traveling from city to city in the Northeast and took on all challengers. He liked to play straight pool and played to win. His last appearance was in south Brooklyn where serious pool players were numerous and tough. But as times before, he devastated the competition. Danny was somehow able to persuade this sensation to visit his poolroom. This would undeniably boost his business even more.

Weeks before his appearance, Danny hung up posters on every light pole and every storefront in the area. It became the talk of the streets. The other business owners all supported it and hoped it would boost their own mediocre sales. Danny's Place would inevitably benefit.

In anticipation of the event, serious local pool players frequented Danny's poolroom daily. They all tried earnestly to improve their game. Some of the players were skillful enough to run the table eight or more times. They could consecutively sink one hundred and twenty balls or more without a missed shot. These men worked their jobs during the day and met nightly to be with other avid players. Their controlled light touch with a cue stick was sometimes amazing and made shots that looked impossible. Playing pool seemed to be an obsession with all the players consistently challenging each other.

As the day came closer to Willie's arrival, the atmosphere intensified with excitement. Among the local players, the one who had the highest run would have the opportunity to challenge the visiting champion.

The day finally arrived, and at three o'clock on a Saturday afternoon, a taxi pulled up in front of Danny's Place. A young man of small stature exited and looked up at the poolroom's façade. The locals had already crowded inside to wait. When he entered, someone yelled out,

"Welcome, Willie!" as everyone clapped their hands enthusiastically. Willie was gracious and expressed his appreciation for being there. After he was introduced, Willie reached for his cue stick case without hesitation. There were racked balls waiting for him on the table. Without fanfare, he gently leaned over to make the break. Three balls instantly found their pockets as he proceeded to quickly clear the table.

Willie set up and executed a series of trick shots that were beyond the spectators' wildest expectations. He continued to captivate this audience for another hour. He finally paused for a break to have something to eat and drink. People around him could not help themselves and asked a barrage of questions regarding his life and his unique talent.

After pausing for half an hour, Willie returned to the pool table. At that time, the local pool player who had the longest run walked forward to challenge the pro. Easy-going Willie accepted and allowed the local man named Matt to make the first break. Matt was confident and hit the cue ball hard with a resounding sharp crack, splitting the racked balls. Two balls instantly rocketed into opposite pockets. He stopped and chalked his stick as he circled the table. Seeing his next shot, Matt hit the ball into a side pocket then methodically sank all the remaining balls. The balls were racked and ready once more. Matt waited patiently then took his shot which scattered the balls, sinking one in the corner pocket. He continued to sink the rest of the balls. His routine of running the table was repeated a third and fourth time as Willie watched. It was evident that he was an experienced challenger as he continued to make perfect shot after perfect shot. This was repeated through the eighth and ninth set.

He sat down for a minute as the tenth rack was positioned for him to resume playing. Once again, he chalked his stick and forcefully hit the cue ball. On this break, he sunk a ball in the far corner pocket. Matt then circled the table and took his next shot, driving it into the side pocket. He walked over and proceeded to hit a ball toward the other side pocket. The ball shot in that direction but just caught the corner and deflected off the rail and missed going in. This ended a run of a hundred and thirty-eight balls. It was an impressive score.

Everyone watching, including Willie, cheered at his extraordinary effort. The balls were racked as Willie chalked his stick and took a drag on his cigarette. He wasted no time, lined up the cue ball, and made the break, sinking three balls to the opposite corners of the table. With the grace of a dancer, Willie walked around looking for his next shot which he took without hesitation, sinking the ball. He swiftly drove one more and then another into a pocket, and before anyone realized it, ran the table. He was more methodical in his next game and deliberately made his subsequent shots with precision. As before, the time passed quickly. The crowded room of spectators made themselves comfortable, for they anticipated an intense and lengthy demonstration.

Willie calmly and skillfully ran table after table. He paused when he reached Matt's total run. He looked directly at Matt and continued to pass his total. Willie shot the remainder of the balls to end the tenth table run.

Willie resumed after a much-needed break. His light touch and accuracy never waned as he extended his run. The veteran pool enthusiasts knew they were witnessing something amazing as Willie shot flawlessly. The interest of the onlookers did not waver, and no one left their seat, for they were observing a master pool player in action and all appreciated the significance of the time and place.

Willie's streak extended to twenty-one tables and was increasing with every shot. By now he had surpassed the inconceivable mark of three-hundred balls sunk. Again he made the break as two balls found their pockets. His next shot was a piece of cake as he put the ball in the corner pocket. There were no open shots remaining. The cue ball was smack against two balls. For him to make this next shot, he had to hit the cue ball without touching the other two. It was a difficult shot, but he had made it a hundred times before. He moved closer but was a little off balance, but he still took the shot. The cue ball made it clear as it hit the intended ball which went toward a side pocket. It looked good, but it slightly angled and hit the edge of the pocket, glancing off. It was over. He had a phenomenal run of three hundred and four balls. The crowded room of spectators stood and applauded the outstanding feat. They would probably never be privy to such a performance again, and that Saturday night at Danny's Place would be remembered for years to come.

Uncertain Horizons

Dominick inevitably moved on with his lackluster life, and things shifted when he was twenty-five. He became acquainted with his friend Jay's younger sister, Aida, and there was synchronicity and an immediate, mutual attraction. Their family backgrounds were similar. The town where Aida and her family lived was located a mere ten miles from Dominick's parents' original home in Calabria. Aida was petite and stubborn; her dark hair was bobbed in the fashion of the times and matched her fiery youth. She had a mind of her own, and she did things her own way. The loss of her father at a very young age toughened her resolve in life and relationships. Aida obviously cared for Dominick but was not always demonstrative. On the other hand, Dominick adored her, and his gentle and caring ways eventually convinced her to take a closer look at their relationship. At every opportunity, he presented her with original poetry; she was flattered that anyone would be inspired by her enough to do such a thing. Both families happily accepted and encouraged their courtship. An added incentive was the fact that all the family members got along famously together. The new couple were engaged within a few months into the courtship, and everyone looked forward to attending a future wedding. The betrothed began to put money aside for the reception and wedding costs. Dominick was still working sporadically as a house painter, and Aida worked at a dress factory.

They were married on a windy day in the fall of 1936 at the neighborhood Catholic church. Aida's fashionable silk bridal train flowed behind her, and Dominick escorted his new bride down the aisle in his dapper tuxedo and then later to a reception back at her parents' house.

After the joyful wedding day, the newlyweds retreated to the quiet of upstate New York for a week's honeymoon and then settled into an apartment above Aida's mother's flat. Aida's bachelor brothers and her younger sister lived with their mother downstairs. Aida's Uncle Ralph lived next door, and her older sister Lena and family resided across the street. To add to the family inclusiveness, Dominick's parents, sister, and brother Carl relocated next door to Lena. Dominick's brother Frank and his wife were also close by. Evidently, half the neighborhood consisted of Dominick's and Aida's relatives. As a result, holidays and birthdays were all celebrated with large, festive gatherings. To add the fun, Jay and his new wife made their home further up the street.

Amidst this close camaraderie, one personality in particular stood out. It was everyone's Uncle Ralph, the self-appointed overseer of the family and entire neighborhood. He shared an apartment with two other Italian men who were also married with families still residing in Italy. Ralph was not an average individual and most unique. He had a wife and two daughters in Calabria but he had decided to come to America to test the waters. After almost a year of living in Brooklyn, Ralph had made up his mind to make a permanent life in the United States. He took a boat back to Italy to talk his wife and daughters into joining him for good. When he arrived in Italy, Ralph spent the next six months trying to convince his family to move. This apparently was a failed effort.

One day, after Ralph had been in Italy for half the year, his nephew Jay happened to walk along the avenue and spotted a familiar figure walking toward him. It was his Uncle Ralph carrying a suitcase. The amiable man hugged Jay and told him he was back for good and informed him that is family refused to come, so he said goodbye and left. He promised them he would work and send them money to live on every month. Jay shook his head and smiled, for he knew his bull-headed, unpredictable uncle.

Ralph wasted little time getting back to interfering in the lives of his relatives, whether they liked it or not. He elected himself protector of his nephews and nieces, though they wondered what they needed protecting from. In addition, he was a notorious gossip of major proportion. He had an uncanny ability to show up at the most inopportune times and had a knack for catching his younger family members in compromising situations. Needless to say, they were all paranoid of their nosy uncle's sudden appearances. All during the week, Ralph's constant surveillance of everyone culminated with his Sunday visits. This was the day he would come knocking and give everyone a verbal dossier on the activities and misadventures of their offspring. While visiting their homes, Ralph was usually offered a shot of liqueur which he accepted too readily. No one took offense of his extreme concern for their welfare. Once Ralph's weekly rounds were completed, the aftereffects of the libations took their toll, and he was barely able to walk back home.

Another one of Ralph's supposed talents included the idea that he was his own dentist. He would attempt to remove a bad tooth by his own hand with a nail. How he survived the pain was mindboggling, but he did. Another attribute he possessed was is unbelievable biting power. On more than one occasion, while everyone cracked walnuts after dinner, Ralph would do the job between his teeth without a nutcracker, to everyone's horror and awe that he actually succeeded. Uncle Ralph would redeem himself, he thought, every Fourth of July. He would put on a grand display of fireworks, for back in his hometown in Italy, he was the town pyrotechnic. He had been in charge of all the fireworks during the celebrated feast days of saints. Least to say, all the kids on Utica Ave. were fascinated by his annual, colorful show.

Jay's brother Lou was another unforgettable character. He was the oldest of the siblings and was a career student.

His interests included languages, philosophy, and politics. The latter almost prevented him from entering the United States. As a student, he was a great supporter of Benito Mussolini's agenda to restore Italy to its former Roman prestige. When Lou arrived on Ellis Island with the rest of his family, the U.S. authorities discovered his books and articles promoting Fascism, and he was refused admittance into the country. He was immediately sent back to Italy. A year later, he came to Ellis Island again, this time sans the Fascist propaganda and was finally allowed to enter America. Upon his arrival at his mother's house, his younger sister Esther and brother Albert read him the riot act about his controversial ideas and opinions. More or less, they told him to keep his mouth shut. But that was not going to happen so easily. He was a free-thinker and spirited intellect who would challenge and approach anyone, regardless of their status.

Lou lived a Spartan existence that did not require much for contentment. The miniscule room where he slept had a narrow bed, a small desk, and scores of books crowded onto shelves. He was satisfied just to read and write news articles. His family did not understand him or his motivations, and he was thought of by many to be an intellectual oddball. It did not faze him, and his lack of response angered his critics. His irreverence for society's sacred cows and its failures were apparent. His integrity was anchored in the truth. This attribute that should have been admired, was scorned, and he continued to live his life the only way he knew how.

Lou applied to Yale University a few months later and

was accepted. He continued his studies but did not graduate because he found the curriculum too rigid for his free-thinking. Regardless of this, he went on to write articles for small newspapers and magazines. One phenomenal example of his intellectual boldness was the time he took umbrage to a statement made by the renowned physicist Albert Einstein. Without hesitation, Lou wrote the famous scientist a scathing letter regarding who received credit for inventing the radio and the omission of any mention of Marconi's contribution. Never thinking he would receive a response, Lou forgot about it. To his amazement, Lou received a letter from Einstein a month and a half later. It was hand-written in German and signed by him. Despite knowing French, Spanish, and Italian, Lou did not know any German. He racked his brain trying to find someone who could translate it.

One night at the supper table, Lou showed the letter to his doubtful siblings. When Jay heard about it, he was amazed as well as his brother-in-law, Dominick. They passed the letter around and examined it. Dominick was struck with an idea when he noticed the box of pastries on the table. He then suggested that he and Lou go to the neighborhood German bakery with the letter.

They approached the owner the next day and presented him with Einstein's letter. He laughed at first and refused to believe it. He thought they were joking until he began to read it. His amused smile soon disappeared from his face and was replaced by an expression of astonishment. Realizing the letter was indeed genuine, the owner of the bakery offered to translate it for Lou. He walked to the back of the store and wrote a translation and re-emerged after twenty minutes. He handed Lou the original letter along with the copy in English. Lou was grateful and expressed his thanks. The baker said it was an honor to do so and asked if he wanted to sell the letter for fifty dollars. Lou graciously refused.

Dominick and Aida worked diligently the following three years to save for a better future. In the fall of 1939, their lives would change forever as Alda gave birth to their first child, a baby boy in early October. Following tradition and out of respect for his father Giuseppe, Dominick named him Joseph. At this time, Aida gladly quit her job to raise her son. Dominick put in as many hours as he could as a house painter to make up the difference.

Signs of war in Europe became more evident with increasing rants by Adolf Hitler. England was building its arsenal and preparing for war. As result, they were relying on American industry to help build ships and other vital military hardware to meet their overwhelming needs. The machine shop where Jay had been working as foreman could not keep up with the orders and needed more workers. Jay thought this would be a good opportunity for Dominick and approached him about the job. To his surprise, Dominick accepted. The painting business was sporadic and not dependable, so Dominick made the change. Aida was happy, for the work was steadier and Dominick would be working alongside her brother.

Conditions in Europe were deteriorating with every week that went by. It appeared increasingly ominous as

Hitler forcibly annexed surrounding countries with impunity. To add to the impending doom, Mussolini joined Germany and Japan and formed an axis pact. German politicians and military leaders ridiculed the helpless nations which they occupied. When the Nazi government was questioned about their takeover of sovereign nations, they claimed it was for the benefit of all German-speaking people. In the U.S., there was an undeniable fear that we would inevitably be sucked into a military conflict. Most Americans did not desire to be involved in a European war, but as nations continued to be overrun, it was apparent that the United States would play an important role. With the looming anticipation of our entrance into a war, men under the age of thirty-five began to speculate about their uncertain futures. Dominick, his brothers, and his friends were no exception.

One afternoon after eating the traditional Sunday dinner, Dominick reluctantly approached his father and said, "Pop, I don't know how to ask you this question," and paused. "It looks as if we might soon go to war. If we fight against Germany, that means we will also be fighting against Italy. Pop, we'll be fighting Italians and in your homeland."

"Basta, enough," Giuseppe stated then asked, "Where were you born and where do you live?" A little surprised, Dominick thought for a moment.

"Here, of course."

"Exactly, my son," Giuseppe emphasized. "Then this is where our loyalty lies. There is no dilemma. You are an American, nothing else." Giuseppe stopped speaking abruptly as his eyes filled with tears. He then walked somberly into the next room. At that moment, Dominick realized the magnitude of his father's patriotism and gratitude for America, despite the fact that someday he or his brothers might fight against family members in Italy.

As millions of others, Dominick—the son of immigrants—would have to face uncertain and precarious challenges. With unyielding perseverance, they would find a way to overcome tremendous odds on their arduous path to final victory and hoped that the future would culminate in a lasting, blessed peace.

Acknowledgements

Thanks to all the characters—family and friends—who made an everlasting impression on my life.

Thank you to my wife Marlaina who rekindled my snuffed-out passion to write and her incalculable assistance and faith in me.

And my dog Noah, for fifteen years of the purest example of loyalty and love.

About the Author

Joe Donato is the author of the historical biographical novel *Saber's Honor*. He was born in Brooklyn, New York and raised in Madison, New Jersey. Despite showing considerable talent in art and having aspirations to be a sculptor, Joe majored in finance with a minor in philosophy and received a degree from Seton Hall. He lives in beautiful rural New Jersey with his wife Marlaina.

See Jos. C. Donato on Facebook
or contact Joe by email: sabershonor@yahoo.com

Visit **Ekstasis Multimedia** www.booksandbrush.net